# OUR ONCE WARM EARTH

# OUR ONCE WARM EARTH

## MATTHEW RASNAKE

*For family.*

This story contains content which may upset some readers.

Specific content warnings may be found on the last page.

# PROLOGUE



*21 August 2048*
*Somewhere above Deadeye Lake*
*Northern California*

THE FIRELIGHT FLICKERED IN MELANIE'S EYES AS SHE LAY BACK against Daniel's chest and looked up at the stars. John remembered long ago when, as newlyweds themselves, he and June had carried on like these two. *Well, not so long ago, really. We were always like that.*

They'd been back from their honeymoon for only a week, and still were always together, seemingly always connected. Daniel put his hand on her belly and she moved it down and to the right and held it in place. A moment later she looked up at him and he smiled and kissed her temple.

In the still contentment of the night, John thought about the twists and turns that had brought him and Mel to this point. More than thirty years ago he'd dragged her dad to cover under a hell-storm of bullets and promised to protect and guide her as if she were his own. He'd kept that promise as well as he could and loved her like a daughter through all the hardship and heartache of their lives. He was proud of the woman she'd become.

Not that he didn't still worry about her. She could certainly take care of herself, but he'd worried over her for half his life and could hardly be expected to stop now.

In the months before the wedding, Daniel's work had taken him away from Mel often enough that sometimes it seemed the two spent more time apart than together. When they'd agreed to come up the mountain with him for the weekend, he'd been excited about the chance to spend time with them as a couple. Now here they were, obviously in love and excited to be together. *Maybe I can give up worrying… a little bit.*

The night grew darker and the air cooler, and John stood and stepped closer to the fire. For a moment he enjoyed the heat, then he circled the fire and walked a few paces away. The moon hid behind the mountain, but the fire and the cloudless, star-filled sky gave plenty of light.

The view over the Deadeye Basin and down the western-facing valley had long been one of June's favorites, and it was as beautiful as he remembered. She had found so much joy in this place.

Behind him, the scrape and crunch of rock suggested Mel was up and headed his way. Discretely, he wiped tears from his eyes.

She stepped up behind him, wrapped her arms around his chest, and lay her chin on his shoulder. His eyes welled, and he squeezed her arms around him and pressed his head against hers. They stood like this for several minutes until she let go long enough to step beside him and wrap her arm around his back.

"I'm glad we're here," Mel said. "It's been too long."

"Me too."

"She really loved this place, you know, but not half as much as she loved you."

"I know." Tears fell on John's cheeks and he made no effort to hide them.

"You okay?"

"Yeah," John said. "Gettin' there."

For a moment, they silently took in the view while John scanned the sky, as he did almost every night, to find one tiny light among the thousands. Mars hung just above the valley's southern ridge among a host of stars.

"Where is she tonight?" Mel asked.

John pointed. "Just above the ridge, there."

"Hard to believe she's been up there almost two years already," Mel said. "Building a home and living their dream."

"June was so proud of her," John said. "Me too, once I got past the fact that she was leaving us forever. First, she and Luis haul my only grandkids off to Mars, then Nick moves to Berkley, and now June's gone and it's just me in that big old empty house."

"Well," Mel said, and squeezed him to her side, "my wandering days are over." She patted her belly gently. "Danny and I aren't going anywhere."

"I'll believe that when I see it," John said. "You've never been one to stay put for long."

"I know," Mel said. "I can't explain it, but I'm finally happy. Before things always felt so confined, but with Danny and with the baby on the way, I feel like there are no limits, like the whole world has just been waiting for us."

John smiled and looked down the valley. Under the starlight, the mountain and the forest below it stretched for miles. It had been a long road, and not always an easy one, but he wouldn't trade a moment of it. "It's a very lucky person who finds just what she needs, just when she needs it," he said and kissed her forehead. "I'm happy for you."

"Don't worry too much about Leana," Mel said. "She's exactly where she always wanted to be."

"I'm happy for her, too," John said. "But I miss her and I can't help but worry. She, Luis, and the boys have had the run of the place for two years, I just hope they're really ready for everything to change."

"What are you two conspiring about over there?" Danny called from the other side of the fire. "These marshmallows aren't going to roast themselves!"

Mel ignored him. "I'm sure they'll be fine. Besides, knowing Luis, he's already fermented half the fruit from their greenhouse." She gave John a wink.

A light breeze carried their laughter up the mountain into the dark night.

# UNDER THE WEATHER

Mel sat on a small boulder near the fire and sucked on her teeth. Nearby, John lay his empty camp dish on the ground, leaned back on his elbows, and soaked up the evening sun like a plumpish flannel-covered cat.

"That was some damned good fish," he said. "Don't know how, but I always forget how good pan-fried lake trout is when you catch it, clean it, and cook it under a clear blue sky." He leaned his head back and let out a great, satisfied sigh.

*Once you get past those annoying pin bones, at least.* "Well, thanks," Mel said, "but I didn't do much apart from frying them up." The baby kicked, and she cupped her belly in both hands. "Hello there, little one," she cooed.

Danny gathered up their metal camp plates and utensils, wiped them down, and carefully sat them on a log near the fire and the boiling pot of lake water he and John had brought back from fishing.

"Don't sell yourself short, kiddo," John said. "That was as fine as anything June ever managed to get out of the pan." He sat up and fiddled with his yellow weather alert radio. "But of course, she hated the damn things. Couldn't stand the smell of them cooking."

A few meters away, Danny rummaged through his pack and pulled out a lightweight jacket.

"Oh, I don't know about that," Mel said. "I've had her cooking too, ya know. I know how good you had it all those years." She threw a bit of tree bark in John's direction and just missed Danny's rear end as he slunk past and grabbed a camp stool.

John didn't talk about June much, at least not to anyone but Mel. He wasn't the type to crow about things that bothered him or to wear his heart on his sleeve, and whenever June came up, he tended to get emotional.

"You certainly aren't wrong there," John's eyes glistened.

The last sliver of sun slipped behind the clouds that rolled over the distant horizon. Gorgeous pinks, purples, and reds stretched across the sky and painted the wispy clouds above the valley. Overhead, the sky was clear and calm—as beautiful as any you could wish for. John watched the sunset for a long moment.

*How many sunsets had he seen like this with June*, Mel wondered. *Twenty-five? A hundred? How many from near this very spot?*

When her dad died, she'd been too little to understand, but John had come home and everything seemed magically okay again. Her mom was sad, but slowly even she woke up again. John and June were an undeniable force in their lives and filled every day with warmth and love.

When June died, Mel stood by him like he'd stood by her every day she could remember. They cried together for days— he'd never seemed so vulnerable. If June's absence felt like someone had scooped out a part of her and not put it back, she couldn't imagine how empty John must have felt. But she worked on him. Gave him little reminders. Tried to fill him back up.

He wiped away tears and flashed her a sad smile.

"So, what's with the radio, anyway?" Mel asked.

"Better safe than sorry," John said. "Danny and I saw a storm brewing out west this afternoon when we were hoofing it back up here. Far off still, but building. Could be trouble, could be nothing. I took the radio down with us this morning to charge and now it should be good for a week of overcast days."

John was endearingly optimistic, but he was also no fool. Mel always suspected that the Army had tempered him in that regard.

Danny dragged his stool near the fire and sat hunched over, hands stretched out as though to draw the flames closer. Something was off about him. Mel scrunched her eyes but nothing jumped out at her. *A little tired, maybe?* He and John had spent the better part of the day fishing by the lake. *Probably just worn out from spending all day in the sun.*

"Feelin' alright, son?" John asked.

The fact that John voiced her own thoughts did little to make Mel feel better.

"Just a little chilly," Danny said. "Got cold all of a sudden."

Though the sun had set, it didn't seem significantly cooler. The fire, perhaps, could use another log, but otherwise, the night was comfortable. Nevertheless, Danny zipped up his jacket, pulled the sleeves over his hands, and shoved them under his tightly crossed arms. His whole body seemed to curl into itself, and he visibly shivered.

"Ok, seriously," Mel asked, "what's going on?"

"Not sure," Danny said. "I think I'm…"

He stood suddenly, knocked over the camp stool, and looked around the campsite in what seemed like a panic. He bolted from the fire and stumbled fifteen or twenty paces away before he steadied himself with one hand on a tree, doubled over, and puked his guts out on the ground.

WITH MORE EFFORT than it would've taken a month before, Mel scrambled to her feet and rushed to Danny's side. She regretted it almost immediately—the smell turned her own stomach. She covered her mouth and nose with her shirt, which did little good, so she just held her nose instead and breathed through her mouth.

"Danny?" She retched but recovered. "You okay?"

He spat a few times, then slowly straightened up. "No," he said quietly, "but a little better now, I think."

Back near the campfire, John hung a bag filled with water they'd boiled while their dinner cooked, and retrieved the camp soap from their supplies.

"John's getting some water ready so you can wash up and rinse your mouth," Mel said. "You ready?"

Danny rested his head in the crook of his elbow for a moment as he leaned against the tree. "Yeah," he said.

He stood a little straighter, and they turned and walked back toward the campfire. Before they got all the way back, Mel stopped him.

"Hang on, before we get too close to the fire…" She put her hand on his forehead, then against his neck under his jaw. "Ooh, yeah, you're definitely warm."

She led him to the water bag and helped him wash his hands and rinse his mouth. She sacrificed one of their hand towels. "This one's yours now, until the trip's over."

"So, son, how're you feeling?" John asked.

"Like shit," Danny replied. "I'm freezing, and my legs ache. I just want to crawl into bed and go to sleep."

"He's burning up," Mel said. "Should we take him home?"

"It's a three-hour hike back to the car," John said. "You up for that, Daniel?"

Danny shook his head.

"The boy needs rest and water." John asked, "where's your water, son?"

Mel found it near where Danny had sat to eat dinner and brought it to him.

"Now, you sip on that for a minute. Mel, grab your stuff and let's get you set up in my tent. If he's got the flu or something, there's no sense you getting sick too, and vaccinated or no, that's a lot more likely to happen if you spend the night cooped up in a tent with him."

"Where are you going to sleep?" Mel asked.

"Hammock," John said, "I'll string it up between a couple trees, and I'll be fine."

Danny swayed on his feet and sipped his water. His jacket was fully zipped with the hood up. He stood a foot or two from the fire and still he shivered.

"I'd feel better if we headed out now," Mel said. "He really doesn't look good, John."

"I'll give him something to knock down the fever so he can sleep. But Mel, if we left now, it'd take us an hour to break camp, and then it'd be you and me carrying all our gear—and maybe Daniel too—down the mountain in the dark. It wouldn't be easy even if you weren't pregnant. Besides, even if we managed to get him home tonight, no doctor's going to see him until tomorrow, and all we could do is give him ibuprofen and put him to bed anyway. He's better off staying here and getting some sleep. We can reevaluate and bug out in the morning when he's rested and we have some light."

"I get it," Mel said. "I hate it, but I get it."

"Alright Daniel, you get ready for bed and we'll get everything situated," John said.

Danny nodded and stumbled off toward the tent. Mel followed him to help and get her things while John got to work.

Danny's boots landed unceremoniously outside the tent.

*Goodnight, sweetie*, Mel thought. After almost half an hour—and a lot of second-guessing on Mel's part—things were mostly situated and Danny was in bed. The fire had died down, but the moon above the eastern ridge behind them flooded the valley with light.

"If you want to go tuck him in, you can," John said. His tone was playful, but not unsympathetic. "I can finish tying this ridge line myself."

"Nah, we're good."

Mel helped John secure his poncho to the line they'd strung above his hammock to provide some cover, then she staked the front guy lines in place while John worked on the back.

Danny had looked a bit off when they'd come back from fishing, but she'd been too preoccupied with her painting of the Basin to really notice. Maybe if she'd been less worried about getting her colors right, she'd have paid more attention to his color being wrong.

"He didn't look too great, did he?" John asked as he came back around to the front of his little shelter.

"Nah. But he's like an ox—hardly anything phases him," Mel said. "And when he does get sick, he doesn't show any signs of it until he just completely goes off a cliff. One moment he's perfectly fine and a few hours later I'm kicking myself for not putting the CDC's number in my phone's favorites the last time."

She and John walked back toward the fire.

"And then," she continued, "he'll greet me in the kitchen the next morning with pancakes and strong black coffee, making me think the whole thing was just a delusion. Hopefully, this'll be one of *those* times."

"I hope so, too." John poked at the embers, which sent sparks into the air. "I'd hate to have to put him down before we get back to civilization."

"Hey!" Mel glared at him as she sat near the fire.

"What, an old man can't tell a joke?"

"Maybe," Mel said. "If it was funny."

"Aw, you know I'm kidding. I'm sure he'll be fine."

"Yeah..." Mel folded her arms, leaned back against her log, and closed her eyes.

Mel was pretty much the opposite of Danny—for her, symptoms would show up the moment a sick person got near her, and then she'd be miserable for a week. All the vitamins and herbal supplements she took never seemed to help.

When she and Danny had decided to try for a baby, he'd convinced her to get all her vaccinations up-to-date and to ask her doc how to shore up her immune system. The doc just said, "get plenty of rest, drink lots of water, and try to eat more natural foods." *Such a help, that one.*

John sat down nearby. "Look, I know I've told you this before, but... I'm proud of you," he said.

"John," she interrupted. He'd switched to his "serious" voice, which usually led to the kind of discussion she wasn't prepared to have out here under the stars.

"No, now, let me be serious for a minute." John held up his hand. "You didn't like my joke, so let me be serious."

*Of course, I've never been able to stop him before.*

When John broke out the serious voice, his whole demeanor changed. His eyes never wavered from the person he was talking to, and his normally steady, strong voice grew quieter and warmer.

"That Daniel is a good kid," he continued. "He's a good, solid kid, and he obviously loves you a lot. And you two are great together."

*So this is the kind of stuff that shakes loose when two dudes snooze, talk, and fish together for hours.* Mel held back a chuckle.

"So, I just wanted to say that I'm glad you've found

someone like my June was for me, and like Scooter was for your mom. That you've found that kind of partner."

It was funny, in a way. John had only once actually said to her: "your dad would be proud," but every time the serious voice came out, that sentiment seemed to color whatever he said. As if, unconsciously, he wanted to tell her the things her dad no longer could.

Of course, the serious voice also came out—and carried equally weighty undercurrents—when she'd disappointed him. *Which, thankfully hasn't happened in a while.*

"Thanks. I'm pretty lucky, I guess," she said. "And I'm really glad that you two get along as well as you do." *Finally.*

Mel got up to retrieve the pot from the remains of the fire and poured a bit of the water off into a second pot. The pot had stopped boiling a few minutes ago, but it was obvious from the rising steam that the water was still too hot to touch, so she sat back down.

She certainly considered herself lucky—Danny was awesome. He was funny, self-assured, and very attentive. Nobody was perfect of course, but his faults were few and minor. She loved how he smelled, and how soft and strong his arms were. It was dangerous, as she could easily lay with him for hours and lose herself in his warmth.

Before Danny, she'd always been happiest on her own, but somehow they'd both arrived at the same place, time, and frame of mind, and fit together. Now she couldn't imagine life without him. Even still, she sometimes didn't let him see it. The stubborn, independent streak that had led to so many of John's past "serious" talks still kept her from relying on Danny as much as she knew she could.

His job often kept him away for days or weeks, and left her time and space to exercise her independence and to really, honestly miss him. He was a buyer for a few major regional restaurant chains and provided antiques and kitsch for use as decoration. Typically, he'd travel to antique stores, estate sales, or hunt for collectors or packrats, but lately, with the baby on the way, he stayed closer to home. It made it harder to find the unique pieces his clients wanted, but Danny was good at his job.

Mel took some vicarious pleasure from his success, but her own ambitions were simple—she'd always been content with a job that paid enough to live on with a little left over to sock away for the future or to buy herself the occasional "want" along with the "need." Overall, her life was pretty damned good. She and Danny were happy, and her mom was healthy and happily retired to her house in Redding. Between his empty nest and June's loss, John was a work in progress, but she intended to keep him close.

Mel got back up, tested the temperature of the water in the pot, retrieved the soap from among the cooking supplies, and started on the dinner dishes and utensils.

The noise nudged John from whatever reverie he'd been in. "Yeah, he's a good kid," John said.

If John was still talking about Danny, the distance of his tone and the direction of his gaze told Mel that he was thinking about Leana. For a hard-ass ex-Army grunt, John was one of the most sentimental men she knew—the thing he cared most about was family.

June's cancer had nearly broken him—it was the only thing he couldn't protect her from. Now his daughter was millions of kilometers away and there was nothing he could do for her if she needed him. He rarely spoke about it, but it ate at him, and he couldn't hide that from Mel.

He stood and stretched. "Well kid, I'm about ready to hit the sack." He helped rinse the last of the dishes, and spread and doused the fire's last embers while she put everything away.

They hugged and said goodnight, and Mel went to check

on Danny. He tossed a bit when she opened the tent, and he was very warm but otherwise seemed peaceful. She crawled back out and zipped the tent up behind her. It would be the first night in months that she and Danny hadn't slept together. *Probably already have whatever he's got, but I guess it's better to not risk it.* She walked the few steps to John's tent.

John carried the weather radio to his shelter and suspended it from a carabiner attached to the ridge line. He looked down the valley. "Don't forget to zip up tight, Mel, this storm may be coming for us after all."

She hesitated for one last moment, then crawled inside the tent and sealed herself in.

# DESPERATE CLIMB

The radio crackled to life, and John snapped awake. The obnoxious alert tone drilled into the side of his skull, and he strained to listen through the resonant noise for clues to what set it off. A light breeze rustled the poncho above him, but otherwise the campsite lay quiet under the moonlight much as it had when they'd gone to bed.

The radio tracked its position and polled for severe weather alerts for the immediate area. Its activation meant something was imminent. The alert slid abruptly into silence and a synthetic voice read a message:

*Hazardous Weather Alert. This alert is for the Shasta-Trinity National Forest and surrounding areas. Regional weather services are monitoring a storm exhibiting unexpected and extreme activity. Predictive models suggest that major thunderstorm activity including lightning, heavy rain, and dangerous wind conditions exceeding one-hundred KPH should be expected to cause flash-flooding and significant damage to trees and temporary shelters. This rapidly developing, fast-moving system is predicted to build over the next one to two hours and enter the area within twenty-five to thirty minutes. Anyone within the alert area is strongly advised to seek permanent shelter immediately.*

John dressed and was out of the hammock before the message ended. He crossed the campsite to his tent, flashlight in hand. Mel's voice came from the direction of her and Daniel's tent, so he ran there and tapped on the fabric near the unzipped door. "Mel, we've got a problem."

"Oh! John, Danny really doesn't seem well."

He knelt down and pulled the door open. Mel sat next to Daniel with her hand on his forehead. Daniel's rosy face glistened with sweat, and he lay fetal with the sleeping bag clutched under his chin. John leaned into the tent and pointed the flashlight up into the roof to spread its light without blinding them.

"I heard him moaning in his sleep, so I came to check on him. He's burning up!"

"I'm fine." Daniel's teeth chattered, and he sucked his breaths in small sips. "Just a little cold, that's all."

John checked his wristwatch. *2am. Six hours, give or take.* "I'll get you more ibuprofen." John said, "but you two need to get up and ready to go."

"What? We can't! Why?" Mel asked.

"That storm is coming our way and has apparently turned ugly. We have to find shelter, **now**. Get dressed, quickly. I'll be back in a sec."

John ran back to his shelter under the light of the nearly full moon, grabbed his pack from the tree where it hung, and ran back with it. He dug his pill bottle out of the side pouch, shook three into his palm, and handed them to Mel.

Daniel took the pills with water from his canteen. "Thanks," he said, and struggled to fish his blue jeans from the bottom of his sleeping bag. John let the door flaps fall closed as Mel helped Daniel get dressed.

Soon, they were all outside the tent, which thrummed with each gust of wind.

"So, what are we going to do?" Mel asked.

"There are several caves nearby that I'm familiar with, one is just up the mountain to the northeast about a mile, mile-and-a-half maybe," John said. "We can hole up there until morning."

"A mile?" Mel looked at Daniel, who nodded. "What about our stuff?"

"Leave it," John replied. "Grab your packs. Leave everything else. We don't have time to break camp, and we'll make better time without it. The tents are staked down, so just zip 'em up and we'll come back this way in the morning to get them, if they're still here."

They secured the tents against the wind as best they could, then Mel helped Daniel put on his pack as John wrestled with his own. Daniel rocked on his feet, every movement followed by a wince and a momentary pause as she fussed over him.

*When did her belly get so big?* With Mel almost five months pregnant and Daniel falling apart, John hoped they'd make it to the cave before the storm rolled in over them.

He untied the poncho and left the cordage, stakes, and his hammock behind. Mel helped him shove the poncho into one of his backpack's side pockets.

Wind rustled through the trees, and John took a moment to get his bearings. To the east the moon and stars shone brightly on the trees and scrub, to the west they disappeared into the impenetrable dark and took the valley and the forests beyond the mountain with them.

The trio headed up the valley and quickly picked up the trail that had brought them to the Basin. John led them along it to the northeast for several minutes while the grade increased and the foxtail and chaparral thinned around them. When the trail turned more northerly, John abandoned it in favor of a more direct route toward the cave. For ten minutes, they skirted ferns and shrubs and fought for footing on the uneven, rocky ground. Then the mountain rose sharply ahead of them, dotted with boulders and scraggly pines. John cursed under his breath.

Already winded, Mel and Daniel struggled to keep the pace. From here, the climb would only get more difficult. Behind them, the trees whistled and moaned, and the sky darkened as the storm strengthened and the clouds swallowed more stars.

*No time for fear,* John thought, then shouted, "We have to keep moving! We're running out of time!"

Mel and Daniel nodded and John hoped that adrenaline would be enough to push them the rest of the way. The ground was loose and steep, and Daniel slipped and fell on his knee.

"Grab whatever you can and climb! Just keep moving!" John paused a meter or so up the slope while Mel helped Daniel to his feet and got him moving again. *She's every bit her father's daughter.*

They pulled themselves along by pine branches, low-lying shrubs, and large rocks until their hands were sticky and bloody. They climbed, slipped, stumbled, and fell. They gasped for every breath, though no one could hear over the awful noise of the wind. John glanced back at almost every step to make sure they were still with him. The ground shook, and John missed a step and stumbled. *Whoa. What...*

"You feel that?" Mel shouted up to him.

The ground shook again, harder this time, and John's heart pounded in his chest. Mel's eyes went wide, and small rocks skittered past. Lightning flashed over the valley behind them.

"Keep moving!" John shouted.

The ground rolled the loose, rocky soil under their feet and threw them to the ground. A crack of thunder pounded John's chest. Another brilliant flash of lightning struck and this time he counted as the blue afterimage faded. Somewhere nearby, a tree crashed to the ground, then the thunder came again and hit him like the IED that had taken out his humvee in Afghanistan. *42 seconds. Jesus. What the hell is going on?*

Mel scrambled to her feet. "Are you sure the cave will be safe?" She struggled to help Daniel up.

John hesitated for a moment, then scuttled back down to them. "There's no choice!" He grabbed Daniel's arm. "Now let's move! We don't want to be out here while these trees are coming down!"

Above them, beyond the spur they'd nearly crested, a diffuse glow momentarily outshone the moon and stars, then slowly faded. Trees swayed in heavy gusts of wind and the ground trembled in a long, low rumble underfoot. Trunks and branches cracked and popped all around them, while small rocks danced down the slope.

A blast of warmth assaulted them from over the spur, accompanied by an impossibly loud sound that stabbed John's skull. He clutched his ears and struggled to keep his footing, but fell back. The sound passed as quickly as it had come, but his ears rang. Mel and Daniel lay crumpled on the rocky ground, hands on their ears, their faces masked with pain.

"What the fuck!" Mel shouted, her voice muffled as though she were underwater.

John grabbed her shoulders and helped her to her feet. She held onto him and cradled her belly as she tried to catch her breath.

"You okay?" John asked.

Mel nodded and squeezed his arm. Daniel was in worse shape, but together they got him up.

They clambered over rock and pinemat, and pulled themselves up the mountain by branch or shrub. At times they met the mountain halfway and climbed on all fours. The rough ground left their hiking pants scuffed and discolored, and their palms and elbows scratched and bloody. Their feet and knees tingled from the constant rumble that rose from deep underground.

The ground leveled out near a rocky outcrop at the ridge of the spur. Wind howled past them, and the storm's first misty raindrops spattered their necks and arms. Darkness had engulfed the valley and nearly overtaken them.

The outcrop was the first finger of a wall of rock that followed the eastern side of the spur and grew several meters tall before it disappeared behind the trees. At its base, a trail led to a cave they had to stoop to enter.

"Here we are," John said.

In the wild moonlit night, the cave's inky blackness offered little reassurance.

A light patter of rocks rained from the cave's mouth as Mel and Daniel limped in together. Overhead, clouds crawled across the stars. The moon rose high above the valley's eastern ridge where brief flashes of lightning illuminated thin shadows. John had never seen such an immense storm move so fast or become so violent. Between the chaos in the sky above and the tremors from the ground below, it seemed the Earth herself wanted to fold them under and swallow them up.

Then in an instant so sudden that his breath caught in his throat, the moon dimmed, flashed bright as the sun, then vanished into utter darkness.

## FADE TO BLACK

"WHAT THE HELL?" JOHN BLINKED AT THE NEWLY DARKENED sky.

"John, get your ass in here!" Mel and Daniel were already a few meters into the cave.

"Mel!" John shouted, "You didn't see that?"

"See what?"

"Come here for a second and look!"

Mel grunted her displeasure. Lightning punctuated the darkness, and she was only visible briefly, flash-frozen in mid-step. She emerged from the cave and gazed into the darkness. "Look at what? I can't see anything!"

"No, not around here..." He put one hand on her shoulder and with the other pointed to where the moon had been. "Out there."

"What? What am I looking at?" She shouted above the wind.

"The moon!"

"What moon?"

"Exactly!" John said. "Mel, there was nearly a full moon tonight."

"It's night. The storm…" She hesitated, "You can't see it through the clouds."

"I could," John said. "I was looking right at it, and it just… crumbled to nothing right in front of my eyes."

Wind and rain whipped past the rock wall and stung his face. Mel seemed to search his face for a moment, then her eyes went wide and she grabbed his arm. "How could that happen? John, what's going on?"

"I don't know, but whatever it is, I don't think we're going to be the ones to figure it out." He unslung his pack from his shoulder and grabbed the weather radio that hung from it. "Let's get out of the weather."

Daniel sat where Mel had left him. He shivered pitifully—the climb had taken its toll.

John took off his jacket and handed it to Mel, who draped it over Daniel. This far into the cave, the wind outside was a dull roar. The ground still thrummed beneath them, and the occasional crack of a tree or branch outside the cave punctuated the relative stillness.

His weather radio reported a weak signal despite its redundant datanet connections and terrestrial radio backup, so he walked it toward the mouth of the cave and tweaked the controls until the signal improved.

Near the entrance, John picked up a handful of twigs and sticks, and a rather large, partially hollow piece of white pine that appeared to have been in the cave for years. With these, he built a small, but respectable fire just beyond the wind's reach. It wouldn't provide much warmth or last very long, but he hoped it would discourage any non-human visitors.

He tried to piece together what they'd seen: a monster storm, earthquakes, aftershocks, some kind of massive explosion, and, as impossible as it seemed, the moon's destruction. No matter how he looked at it, all he knew for sure was that he had no idea what the hell was going on, but he was damned sure whatever it was, wasn't good.

The radio squawked out two long dolorous tones John had never heard before, then began a new message that echoed through the cave:

*General Global Emergency. This is a general global emergency. A catastrophic event presenting a serious, global threat to life has occurred. The exact nature of the event is unclear, however, global flooding, widespread electrical storms, and unprecedented seismic and volcanic activity have resulted in significant loss of life. Resulting clouds of smoke and ash are likely to cover the planet, reducing global temperatures and rendering the planet uninhabitable.*

Behind John, Mel struggled to her feet and came toward him.

*Global governments are issuing shelter-in-place orders for all citizens. However, if you are receiving this message, you are in the vicinity of a government facility designed to provide long-term shelter during national or global emergencies. The shelter will remain open until 10 am PST, after which time the doors will be sealed. The coordinates for this facility, which are being transmitted to your device, are as follows: 35 degrees 25 minutes 30.1 seconds north by 116 degrees 53 minutes 23.1 seconds west. Your device's emergency beacon mode will activate when this message ends and will guide you to the shelter. Again, this is a General Global Emergency. You are in mortal danger and should immediately seek shelter at the provided coordinates.*

The speaker went silent, and an indicator on the radio flashed to confirm receipt of the coordinates.

John and Mel stared at each other for an eternity of seconds, their faces slack. Neither spoke. Slowly, Mel's eyes narrowed, the corners of her mouth twitched, and she erupted in a fit of laughter.

"Mel," John said, "I think that was serious. I think that was for real."

"I know!" Mel gasped. "I know! This is terrible! But, y'know after all this time, all the doomsayers and death cults predicting the end of the world... It's finally happened!" She cackled uncontrollably.

The ground rumbled, then fell quiet. Outside, the storm howled. Mel's laughter died away and her eyes glistened, wet with tears. "Mom..." she said.

John touched her arm. "Sweetie, if things are as bad as that message said, we can't help her. But she would want you to be safe." He lifted her chin, and she met his eyes. "If there's a chance we can make it to that shelter, we have to try."

She dried her face and nodded.

John pulled Daniel's canteen from his pack and offered it to him. "You heard the report, son. Drink up. You look like hell, but we have to move."

Daniel held up his hand to refuse the canteen. His arm trembled, his red-rimmed eyes barely opened, and his breath rattled and wheezed in his chest.

"No," he said. "You go. I'll stay. You come back when the storm passes."

"Danny, no," Mel said. "Drink the water. I'm not leaving without you."

Daniel lay his head back on the rock and closed his eyes.

John put a hand on Mel's shoulder, and when she turned her frightened, angry face his way, he jerked his head toward the mouth of the cave. They walked a few feet away from Daniel and spoke in hushed tones.

"Mel, we have six hours to find this shelter, or we're done. I don't know how far away it is, or in what direction, but there's no easy route to anywhere from here. Wherever we have to go, whatever we have to do to get there, it won't be easy. But if they're right, and we stay here, we're dead."

"I'm not leaving Danny."

"I understand, sweetie, but he can barely walk. Even if we push him, we still might not reach the shelter, and—in this weather, in his condition—he might never recover. If we take him, it's a huge risk."

"I'll carry him myself if I have to."

"You're in no condition either. Would you risk the baby to save him?"

"Yes."

John sighed and rubbed his forehead, then took another breath. "I promised your dad I would watch out for you, that I would protect you. I will not let you die out here, do you hear me? I will get you to that shelter if I have to tie you down and drag you there."

"I'm **not** leaving Danny."

"Mel," Daniel wheezed, "Listen to him. Just go. You won't make it with me."

Mel walked over and kneeled next to Daniel. She smoothed the hair on his forehead, then touched the back of her hand to his neck.

"No," she moved her hand to cradle his cheek, "**We** won't make it without you."

John recognized that determined tone. Nothing he said or did now would change her mind—so either they all went, or none of them did.

"Okay," John sighed. "Mel, empty your packs of everything but the essentials. Pack whatever food and water you have, and a dry change of clothes and an extra pair of socks for both of you. Then put on your rain gear and help Daniel into his—the storm has caught us."

John picked up the radio, and a circle of lights flashed red in sequence. He touched it, and it stopped. Inside the circle, the display flashed *5.0+*, then shifted to the pattern of an arrow that pointed deeper into the cave. They would have to head outside and follow it from there as best they could.

John kneeled next to Daniel as Mel worked to empty their packs. "Son, you heard the report. We've got maybe six hours to reach the shelter before they close the doors and leave us out here to deal with… whatever it is that's going on. Mel won't leave without you, and I won't leave her here. So, I know you're struggling, but you're going to have to dig deep if we're going to have a chance." John leaned in close enough for only Daniel to hear, "I will do whatever I have to to get her through this, even if it means leaving your ass on the side of the mountain. She'll never forgive either of us if it comes to that, but you're not going to let that happen, are you? When this is all over, she's going to need you there. And you **will** be there for her, and for the baby, you got it? Now, on your feet." John offered his hand.

Daniel nodded and took it, and, with some difficulty, stood.

"Mel?" John said.

Her eyes betrayed concern and fear, but also determination. It was the same look her dad had worn every time they'd gone out expecting a fight, and somehow it felt right. She was ready.

"Here," she held out his pack. "All sorted."

In his memory, Scooter's voice echoed, *I've got your back.*

They helped Daniel and each other put on rain gear, then slung their packs over their shoulders. John picked up the weather radio and walked to the mouth of the cave.

"Let's go."

## NO EASY WAY

OUTSIDE THE CAVE, THE WIND HAD CALMED SOMEWHAT, though the storm still raged overhead and dark clouds choked the sky.

It was into this hell that they flung themselves. Rain stung and blinded them. Lightning rained down and thunder rolled across the sky. All around them, trees lay at odd angles. Across the valley, on the eastern slope, fires burned and smoldered among downed trees.

From the mouth of the cave, they followed the rock wall across the spur it sprang from.

"How far?" Mel shouted to John over Danny's shoulder.

John held up his open hand, then pointed straight up the wall. He didn't break stride.

*Five kilometers? That doesn't seem too bad.* Their hike into camp —just under five kilometers—had taken a little more than an hour. *Maybe an hour and a half, then?*

Lightning flashed, and the clap of thunder pounded her head and echoed off the rock wall. Up ahead, John ducked under a fallen tree that leaned against it. *So, maybe a little longer.*

They hadn't walked five minutes before the rock wall disappeared into the mountain and left them in the forested valley spattered with scrub, rocks, and pine. They followed the hint of a path that grew fainter under the barrage of light, sound, wind, and rain, and that became nearly impassable where fallen trees blocked the way. Every so often, John glanced at the radio's indicator. It wasn't long before they'd lost the path altogether, and each step became a struggle to find a way through.

Motivated by pelting rain, lightning that nipped at their heels, and the promise of death if they moved too slow, they pushed themselves across the mountain as fast as they could. Whenever Danny stumbled, Mel was there to help.

Maybe a half-hour after they'd left the cave, John checked the radio again and looked up the mountain. He scrambled over another fallen tree and cursed loud enough to be heard over the storm.

Danny was halfway over the tree when the vibration under their feet swelled to a tremor. He struggled to keep his balance, and Mel rushed forward to help. "How are you doing?"

"Still here," he said, barely audible over the din. He looked exhausted. "The hell is going on? I mean, it doesn't make sense."

"It's the end of the world, Danny."

He sagged against her shoulder and chuckled. "It sure seems that way, doesn't it?"

---

MEL DROVE one foot in front of the other, as lightning illuminated nightmare images in brief flashes—columns of smoke, a wall of water, swaths of downed trees, and an impenetrable blanket of black clouds. The chaos obliterated all sense of time, but she guessed it had been less than an hour since they'd left the cave.

Despite their slow, steady progress, John cursed louder every time he looked at the radio. Danny had kept his feet under him thus far, but fatigue had caught up with him. Every obstacle seemed determined to stop him, but Mel was always right there to help. Still, he hadn't complained or asked to rest since they'd set out. *Don't know if I'd have the heart to push him like this if he wasn't willing.*

John spat out a lengthy stream of expletives and turned to yell back to them. "Keep your eyes open for a path leading up the mountain! We've got to go over! We need a shortcut!"

Only a few steps later the mountain rose sharply on their left, funneled them downward, and effectively cut off any hope of an easy ascent. A nearby rocky outcrop formed a shallow pocket, which John led them to huddle under as best they could.

"Take a load off for a minute." John helped Mel squat down and maneuver into a seated position as far back as she could get. "Got to figure out where we are."

She breathed heavily and ran her hands over her belly under the poncho. "What's the problem?" she asked. The baby fluttered like a fish. *A brief break would be nice—as long as I can still stand and walk after.*

"The problem is we've been hiking over an hour and we've not made any progress." He held up the radio to show the indicator that read 4.8 and pulsed to the arrow that still pointed straight at the mountain. "The shelter must be on the other side of the mountain. It seems we've just been going in a big circle around it."

"Down the drain," Danny mumbled.

"So we keep going, right?" Mel asked. "We get around to the other side and we're good."

"At this rate, we won't make it in time." John handed Mel his flashlight, unslung his pack, and pulled out a worn, laminated military elevation map and a grease pencil. Mel smiled at the echoes of something he'd done dozens of times when she was a kid and he'd taken the family on "adventure hikes" in almost every restored national park.

"My old LT sent me a bunch of these after June and I started camping out here," John said as he unfolded the map. "Said maybe they'd come in handy, and the Army wouldn't miss 'em, anyway."

John oriented the map and quickly figured out their general location. Rain dripped onto the map from the pinemat that overhung their small alcove. He picked up the radio and retrieved the coordinates, which he wrote in the map's margin.

"Now," he said, "let's see if I can remember how to do this."

He studied the coordinates and the map, added marks along the sides, and finally circled a single grid square with the pencil.

"That's where we're headed." The circle encompassed a valley north of the peak where contour lines snuggled up close in a repeating "U" shape that extended around a lake. "And here," he traced his finger around several grid squares on the mountain's south side, "is roughly where we are."

He studied the map for another moment, then stepped out of their meager shelter and back into the pelting rain. Lightning flashed over the valley and thunder rattled their teeth. He scanned the mountain, then ducked back in next to Mel.

"Damn it!" He held the map under her light. "Can't make out a damned thing out there." He placed his finger on the map just above a group of lakes that Mel assumed was about where their campsite had been, then traced a line that followed the contour of the mountain. "We're probably somewhere within these grid squares, but with all the debris out there pace counting was useless, and without recognizable features... damn it!"

"What about your radio?" Mel asked.

"The radio? Of course!" He reached for it, and the arrow pulsed. He paged through a few info screens before he found the coordinates, wrote them on the map, and circled the indicated grid square.

"There we go. That's where we are." He tapped the map with the pencil. "Now…" He bent over the map again, and after another minute had placed a small 'x' inside each of the circled squares. "There. Each square is a kilometer, but if I've done this right, these 'x's should be within fifty to a hundred meters of our coordinates."

Mel traced her finger from one 'x' to the other. "So, we know where we're going, now we just need to head for the shelter from here."

"Trying to get there directly would take us up and over this peak," John tapped the map, "but if we double-back just one kilometer and make for this saddle," he tapped the map again at a different spot near the first, "we should have an easier climb and bypass the peaks altogether. Plus, it will put us on the other side just above this gentler slope that funnels right down toward the shelter."

Mel checked her watch, then glanced at Danny. "Do we have time? Can we still make it?"

"It'll be close. Normally, I'd say we have plenty of time, but we don't know what we're going to find on the way up to that saddle, or on the other side of the mountain. All we can do is try." To Danny he said, "you got any more in you, son?"

"I'm fine," Danny said, though he shivered and hugged himself under his poncho.

"You sure?" Mel asked.

"'m not gonna let you die here," he slurred, "we'll get there even if it kills me."

"Don't you worry, son," John said. "you're not dead yet. What about you, Mel? You ready?"

The baby had quieted, and she'd regained her breath, but

her left calf had cramped. "Yeah, I need to get moving, before I can't."

John nodded and slung his pack over his shoulder, then helped her up. Together, they pulled Danny up between them and left the relative shelter of the outcropping behind.

They retraced their steps and cleared familiar obstacles for fifteen minutes until they reached a downed tree that Mel could hardly get her leg over.

"I swear, this tree did not give me this much trouble before." She kneeled to look, but there wasn't enough room to crawl under either.

"The ground is higher on this side," John said. "Daniel, give her a boost, son."

Danny kneeled so Mel could step up on his knee and swing her leg over the trunk. She straddled it and offered her hand to give him a little extra leverage as well. They hopped down and continued on.

"Don't know if this is getting harder, or if I'm just getting tired… er." Her head swam in the wet, strobe-lit darkness. The mountain rose to her right and fell away on her left, which made it hard to keep her balance. She thought about the warm, soft bed she'd left at home and would probably never see again.

Steps ahead of her, Danny stumbled but stayed upright, and kept only a meter or so behind John despite his obvious fatigue.

More quickly than she'd expected, John stopped and looked up the mountain. "Here," he said, "I think we should start heading up here."

Except in brief flashes afforded by lightning but obscured by steady rain, they couldn't see more than a few meters up the mountain. And what they could see wasn't exactly reassuring—downed trees lay all around on a slope that Mel knew would quickly sap whatever strength they had left.

John glanced at the radio, then at his watch. "Four point eight kilometers," he said. "And just over four hours to get there. You two ready?"

Danny looked as beaten down as Mel felt, but his slack posture said that he felt even worse than he looked. Still, he surprised her. "Yeah," he said, and somehow stacked his body back into some semblance of shape and shambled up the mountain.

She and John shared a look—apparently, they'd both underestimated him.

Danny started strong, and Mel and John scrambled up the rocky mountain after him. The slope was steep, the ground and tree cover sparse, and the rain relentless. Mel slipped on the wet rocks despite her heavy boots, and the others fared little better. After maybe a hundred meters, she ventured a look back. *Okay, maybe more like sixty.*

From here, the slope eased and allowed them to climb in a more upright fashion. Lightning punctuated the darkness. They had to proceed with considerable caution or risk a misstep on a fist-sized rock and a twisted ankle, or worse.

John had never quite given up his old Army habits, which kept him fit for his age and made him cautious in a free sort of way that Mel had always admired. No stranger to this environment, he seemed to push ahead without hesitation and never to step out of place. Occasionally the mountain deceived him and his foot would slip or the rocks give way under him, but still he would barely stumble.

Danny, on the other hand, climbed like a drunk failing a sobriety test. His arms flailed and though he took seconds to decide where to place each step, he still stumbled or slipped almost as often as he didn't. Mel was convinced that it was only his longer legs that allowed him to stay ahead.

After a time, they'd climbed high enough that the trees grew thin, short, and scraggly, and the ground became relatively barren. Lightning revealed the mountain rising away, not just ahead of them, but on either side as well. That reassured them they were where they wanted to be—headed toward a low point in the ridgeline above. The slope grew steeper as they climbed, and once again they had to fight to stay upright or clamber up on hands and feet.

Danny slipped and fell. He tried to raise himself, but slumped back to the ground.

"John!" Mel shouted.

They scrambled to Danny's side.

"Leave me." He said, his voice weak and all but lost in the wind. "I'm finished. Can't go any farther." He shivered violently. "I love you, Mel."

John took Danny's hand and grabbed his elbow. "Kid, you have **got** to stop watching all those damned old movies!" He motioned for Mel to get his other side. "Help me get Mr. Drama King here on his feet."

They pulled Danny up, draped his arms over their shoulders, and carried him up the mountain. Together they struggled against the slope, the wind and rain, and each other.

They climbed like this for a half-hour. They slipped. They stumbled. They fell. They cursed the mountain and the storm and the Earth herself, but each time they picked each other up to take another coordinated step. Their knees and hands were bloody and their rain gear torn and tattered.

Finally, the dull orange glow beyond the ridgeline seemed near enough to touch. With the crest maybe twenty meters away, the ground leveled off and Mel forced herself upright. They'd made the saddle. There was no more mountain to climb.

From where they stood on the ridgeline, lightning revealed the mountain's north slope that fell away below them. The storm had left carnage behind them, but it was nothing compared to their glimpses of what lay ahead.

In the distance, to the northeast, a pillar of black smoke spewed from the nearest mountain while orange fire danced and crawled down her slopes. Destruction radiated from her billowing peak like something Mel remembered only from old photos in history class. The northern sky was black as pitch, the eastern sky choked with haze. The mountain lay quiet under a sun that struggled to filter through that oppressive, smoke-stained sky. At the treeline a few hundred meters below them, almost every tree had fallen, their trunks pointed up the mountain away from the oozing fire, covered by a blanket of snow.

*The shelter is probably destroy… No, Can't think like that. This has to work. We are going to make this.*

"Jesus," John said.

Danny hung between them as they took in the scene.

On the downslope, they made better time. They had to watch to maintain their footing, which Danny's mostly dead weight made harder. As they descended, they found everything covered with a thin layer of fine, dry dust that tickled Mel's throat. The storm—or at least the rain—hadn't made it over the mountain.

She coughed and zipped her jacket collar up over her mouth and nose, while John pulled his shirt over his. They helped Danny lean against a fallen tree while they rummaged through their packs. Mel pulled out the beautiful flower-print headscarf her mom had given her to wear while she painted. She tied it around her head and grabbed another one for Danny. John fashioned something for himself from a bandana, and Mel secured the second scarf for Danny, and tucked the free end into his undershirt.

John checked the indicator on his radio, then his watch. "Three kilometers," he said. "Just under two hours left. We can do this."

Mel helped John get Danny back to his feet. She looked out

over the valley below and to the east, where the ash-choked sun seemed tiny and cold. In its dim light, the landscape was beautiful and terrifying and desolate and sad.

*If this **is** the end of the world, at least it looks the part.*

# THE OTHER SIDE



Mel ached to remember her animated description of the once gorgeous view that now lay twisted and broken below them. As far as she could see, trees lay like reeds bent and broken in a flood. The distant mountain spewed dark clouds that seemed as heavy as the earth itself. The gray choked sky, the gray covered ground, the chill in the air, and the tiny blue sun all piled up on her chest until she wondered how much more she could take. She put one foot in front of the other as John had taught her, and urged Danny on.

The draw down the mountain opened onto relatively level ground—the dust shrouded remnants of a once-lush mountain meadow like the one she'd painted yesterday above Deadeye Lake. As the sun rose higher, even Danny seemed to perk up. Beside them, John checked his radio and excitedly held the display out for them to see. Its indicator pulsed *1+*.

*Holy shit, we might actually make it!*

It seemed so abstract and unbelievable—a storm, whipped up by some nameless tragedy, had driven them from their comfortable night in the woods and sent them running for their lives. Mel tried to keep her eyes, and her mind, focused on her next footstep. She'd have time to figure out exactly what the hell was going on once they reached the shelter. They'd pushed so hard to get this far. She hoped Danny would still be strong enough to recover.

The back of Mel's neck tingled weirdly a moment before she registered the scrape and rustle of footsteps from somewhere beyond where the meadow funneled back onto the mountainside. John heard it too, and pointed out two people fifty or sixty meters below them, coated in gray, their faces covered. One of them angrily waved off the other's hand as they scrambled to get their leg, which appeared to be bound or splinted, over a fallen tree.

"Hello!" John called out.

The newcomers seemed startled and searched for the source of the voice.

"Up here!" John waved his arm.

The uninjured one saw him and waved back, but their companion said something that dragged the pair into an animated argument. The injured one threw up an arm as the other turned, waved to John again, and resumed their climb. A moment later, the injured one hobbled after on some kind of crutch.

John, Mel, and Danny continued ahead to where their path and the newcomers' would cross, and watched their progress. John stopped when the pair was a few yards away and asked, "You heading for the government shelter?"

"Yeah," the friendlier one replied through ragged breaths and tattered flannel.

"Good," John said as he helped the other one over a fallen tree. "I think we have just over an hour to find the shelter before they shut the doors."

Once clear of the tree, the injured one shuffled up on his makeshift crutch, and his eyes darted under furrowed brows from one of them to another, as if he expected a challenge. He huffed and glanced at his watch, then limped off toward the shelter. "Let's go."

His companion shrugged and followed. They mumbled to one another quietly as they walked, and occasionally glanced back at Mel and Danny.

She pulled Danny closer.

***

THE LONGER THEY WALKED, the more Danny fell apart. His body was a furnace against Mel's side, and he stumbled and dragged his feet. Mel's legs trembled and her head swam as she sucked air through her moist, dust-caked scarf. She couldn't afford to indulge her exhaustion. Not for herself, not for the baby, and not for Danny. As close as they might be, he'd never make it on his own.

The newcomers stayed in front, kept their distance, and offered no help. They spoke in whispers, and the injured one continued to regard Danny with an expression that made Mel hold him tighter.

After a lengthy, quiet, but animated exchange, the friendlier of the pair slowed to let John catch up while his buddy grumbled and limped on ahead.

"I'm Nolan, by the way." He addressed all three of them. "DeMarcus. And my curmudgeonly friend up there is Tom."

"I'm John, and this is Mel and Danny."

"Glad to meet ya." Nolan shook John's hand. "I apologize for Tom. We **were** a party of three, camping out on the mountain when, well..." his voice caught, "the trees came down around us. Tom got messed up pretty bad and Grant..." his eyes welled with tears and he glanced at Tom, who wavered a moment then stiffened, lifted his chin, and walked on. Nolan struggled to get out the words. "… our buddy Grant didn't make it. It's been a rough night."

"For us too," John said, "though not as bad, it sounds like. I'm sorry about your friend."

"Thanks," Nolan said, and looked back over his shoulder and down the mountain.

*They left him back there.* Mel considered Tom's dark mood from this new perspective. *I'd be pissed too, if we'd have had to leave someone behind.*

"Tom's leg looks pretty well taken care of," John said. "You EMT, military, something like that?"

"Nah, I'm, er… was an ER nurse at the hospital just north of here."

Danny stumbled and nearly pulled Mel down with him.

"Shit!" Her side burned, but she got Danny righted. *That's gonna hurt tomorrow.* She held her tender side and felt the baby push against her hand. *Along with everything else.*

John excused himself and dropped back to help. "Boy," he said, "you don't look too good." He got under Danny's other arm, and Danny groaned and shuffled his feet to stay upright between them. "Just a little farther now, son." John's somber tone was like a last rite.

Mel fought back tears. *Breathe. Step. Keep moving.*

THE LONGER THEY WALKED, the more their group grew. Twelve others now walked with them. A few were campers like themselves who'd gotten caught out in the storm, but several came from a small, isolated neighborhood a short way down the mountain. Everyone gave their trio wide berth except Nolan, who examined Danny on the move while he peppered Mel with questions.

"If I had to guess," Nolan said, "it's likely viral, maybe flu, but with the stress, fatigue, and no sleep, it's hard to tell for sure."

"Thanks," Mel said, "I'm glad you're here. Who knows what kind of medical care there'll be at the shelter."

Normally, Danny would recover from something like this in a few days, but at the moment, with him barely conscious and suspended between them, she wasn't even sure he'd make it through the night.

The group skirted an outcrop and heard the unbelievable but welcome sound of people somewhere nearby. They picked up their pace almost reflexively until they threaded through an opening into a clearing at the base of a cliff.

It was an incredible, chaotic sight. A few military vehicles sat at one end of the clearing. Some were empty, while people still streamed out of others. Hundreds of people milled about or stood in lines where they waited to pass through checkpoints at three giant steel and concrete doors—*if such massive things can really be called doors*—that were set into the cliff face. People of all ages were in various states of dress or distress. Many of the injured appeared to have received at least basic first aid. Most were quiet, but some screamed or cried despairingly, while others just screamed at anyone or everyone.

Soldiers in forest camo who walked the clearing tried to maintain order and direct newcomers toward the checkpoints, while others processed people through them and into the shelter.

Most of the group they'd arrived with quickly dispersed into the crowd, but the clearing was so full that Mel's feet didn't seem to want to move. John, however, barely slowed down, so with Danny between them, she had to recover her steps quickly to not drag them all to the ground.

A soldier approached the remnants of their group and spoke to Nolan, who motioned Tom over. They talked briefly, then Nolan squeezed Tom's shoulder and headed directly for a checkpoint.

Tom nodded back toward Mel and Danny as he spoke to the soldier who looked them over with an unfriendly, but otherwise inscrutable expression.

## DAY ONE

### San Diego

*8am, 23 August 2048*
*Navy Pier*

DARKNESS. DISTANT CLOUDS OF ASH BLOCK THE EASTERN SUN. *Beyond the quiet bay to the south, Coronado Island smolders and smokes, traces of humanity all but washed away.*

*Debris chokes the otherwise empty Navy Pier. The few cars that remain lay crushed against the parking structure's west face like so much driftwood. The south side, demolished and crumbling, has partially fallen into the bay along with parts of the broken pier where the U.S.S. Midway had berthed.*

*The carrier herself lies two-hundred meters inland, embedded in the remains of the Navy building, her broken flight deck suspended over the bay. The wreckage of planes from her decks lie around her, mixed with debris and bodies washed inland from Coronado or pulled bayward from the city.*

*San Diego, inundated by the tsunami which tore the Midway from her moorings, hosts a handful of bedraggled survivors, huddled on roofs or wandering the futile streets in search of others less fortunate than them-*

*selves. Some scurry about while their recording devices hover nearby, streaming the destruction and their despair onto the global data net.*

# DON'T FORGET ME

THE SPECIALIST—JOHN COULDN'T MAKE OUT HIS NAME TAPE from where he stood—continued to watch them after Tom had hobbled away. He spoke with apparent deliberation to no one in particular, which might have seemed strange if not for the small device and sensor patch he wore on his neck—a throat mic that modern troops used for discrete field communications. The soldier cocked his head like a dog hearing its master's whistle. He'd gotten his answer, whatever it was.

Mel tugged on John's arm. "I think we need to go this way." The tension in her voice confused him, but the way she glanced at the solder while she pulled Daniel toward the nearest line made her worry clear.

*Should've thought about that.* John had been out of the Army for a while, but not so long that he'd forgotten. From first impressions, this seemed like a relatively normal refugee camp operation. He hadn't considered how it might appear to a civilian. *Even an old Army brat like Mel.*

"It's okay, Mel. Take it easy. We're safe."

The specialist made no move to intercept, though his eyes stayed fixed on them. Before they'd crossed the twenty meters to the back of the line, six people in hazmat gear emerged from the crowd behind him, headed in their direction.

Mel adjusted herself under Daniel's arm and pulled him closer to her. She was so agitated she practically vibrated—she was about to rabbit and drag him along with her if she could.

John put his hand on her back. "Don't run. Stay calm."

She relaxed somewhat, then the suits had them surrounded.

"Please proceed to the southern gate." The nearest of the six pointed toward the leftmost door.

John pressed Mel's back gently. "Let's go, kiddo."

She followed his lead and the three of them, surrounded by the yellow suits, set off for the door. Nearer the entrance, it became clear they were headed toward a door in some kind of translucent plastic temporary structure. At the door, two other yellow suits helped an older man through.

"John," Mel stiffened and slowed, "I don't like the looks of this."

"Me either, kid, but I don't think we have much choice."

Two layers of wide, plastic strips served as a sort of door, which then led up a ramp and into a tunnel three or four meters long. Huge overhead fans sucked air past them, through the grated floor, and out of the tiny enclosure. At the other end of the tunnel was another airlock door similar to the first, through which they came out into a large room filled with people. Their escorts directed them to seats along the perimeter of the room.

It seemed everyone here not in protective gear was ill or injured, or in the company of someone who was.

A few folding tables, stacked with paperwork, sat at the far end of the plastic-walled room, where more of the yellow-suits sat or stood. They would call individuals or groups of refugees up to a table, question them, then send them through a door in the back wall.

*Processing.* John had seen similar setups enough times in his career, though even in the worst of those there'd been hope. *Hngh. Fatigue's getting the better of me.*

John and Mel helped Daniel to a seat, then Mel took off her backpack and melted into the seat next to him. She sat the backpack on her lap, crossed her arms over it, and laid her head on them. Her eyes fluttered closed.

Most of the injuries were traumatic—from cuts to broken bones—but very few had received treatment beyond gauze pads and medical tape.

"I heard the worst of 'em'r left outside." The man next to John hadn't so much leaned in as toppled closer. He was dusty with ash, with dark rivulets running from his ears down his jaw and neck where blood and ash had congealed. He held his hands and forearms, similarly stained, out in front of him as though his muscles had all contracted at the same time. His bloodshot eyes echoed around John's head and dragged up half-forgotten memories of old friends. "I heard," the man jabbed a crooked finger in Daniel's direction, "if they can't fix you," his voice broke and rose from a hollow rasp to a tittering sing-song, "they throw you back."

"You there." The person behind the rightmost desk waggled a finger at them.

"Yes?" John replied, and patted Mel on the shoulder.

"You two come here and bring him with you."

John stood and waited for Mel to collect herself and help Daniel to his feet. They supported him and approached the table together.

At the next table, a couple nervously answered questions. Like most everyone else, they were covered in ash and bandages and clung tightly to one another.

"C'mon you three, we don't have all day."

John and Mel helped Daniel sit, then took their own seats on either side of him.

The yellow-suited figure on the other side of the table was virtually indistinguishable from any of the others, but his face, partly visible through the face shield, suggested exhaustion.

"Not very polite, are you, Mister?" John said.

"It's Lieutenant, sir," the man replied.

*Hmph. Lieutenant. Of course.* "Well, Lieutenant," John said, "it seems like your manners need to catch up with your rank."

"Forgive me if I don't roll out a red fucking carpet. It's a little chaotic if you hadn't noticed."

"That's no excuse," John said. "Why did your men drag us in here?"

At the next table, the couple stood and were escorted through the door.

"Your friend here is obviously ill," he said, his yellow finger pointed at Daniel. "If you understood the nature of this shelter, you might also understand how critical it is that we identify and isolate anything that might compromise the safety of the refugee population."

"Refugee?" Mel repeated, her voice slurred by exhaustion.

From behind the door, a female voice shouted in apparent distress. The lieutenant ignored Mel's question.

"Names?"

"Sergeant John Hoffstead, retired. And this is Mel Barber and her husband Daniel," John said.

The lieutenant scribbled their names on his form and asked, "How did you come to this shelter?"

"We were camping and fishing near Deadeye Lake on the other side of the mountain," John replied. "My radio alerted us and directed us to the shelter. The warnings were dire enough that we decided to risk crossing the mountain in the storm." He paused, then asked, "What **is** the nature of this shelter?"

Again, the lieutenant ignored the question. "Was your friend sick before your trip?"

"Not that I knew of," Mel said. "He seemed fine until last night."

"And you two?"

"Aside from being hungry and exhausted, I think it's safe to say we're both all right at the moment," John answered.

"You said Mr. Barber didn't seem sick until last night?" the lieutenant asked. "What were his symptoms then?"

"He said he was tired and went to bed early," Mel said. "I didn't think much of it at first, but when I went to bed later, he had a temperature."

"Hm." The lieutenant ticked some items on the form and scribbled a note. "Vaccinations up to date?"

"Yes," Mel said, "I believe so."

"Yes," John said.

He made more tick marks on the paper. "Corporal," he gestured to two other suits, who stood next to the door. They stepped over to the desk. "Escort these people through." He removed two copies of the form from his clipboard and handed them over.

"Lieutenant," John said, "You didn't answer **my** question. What is this place?"

The soldier who took the form looked it over, nodded, and handed the second copy to his buddy.

"Sir, this really is not the time for questions, but out of respect for your service, I will tell you that you are being processed into the Northern California Emergency Sequestration Facility—one of four command, communication, and survival shelters maintained by the US Army. Our mission, in short, is to preserve and protect our nation and its people. Is that clear enough, Sergeant, or do you need to waste any more of these people's time?" The lieutenant indicated the room with a sweep of his hand.

"No, that's good, thanks."

"Then please, follow the corporal to processing."

Mel and John stood and gathered their backpacks.

The corporal called for a third soldier, who helped pull Daniel to his feet. The corporal led them through the hanging plastic door, while the other two carried Daniel after them.

In the short tunnel beyond the door, six more yellow suited soldiers stood by three doors—two behind where they'd entered, and two each posted beside two other doors. Their escort led them past the first door, and John almost missed the moment the other two diverted and carried Daniel through it.

"Hey! Where are you taking Danny?" Mel shouted, and turned to follow them.

The two guards at the door blocked her. "You can't go through here, Ma'am."

"Why not? Get out of my way!" She tried to shove past them, but they held her off—in her exhausted state, she hardly stood a chance.

"Young man," John said, "you had best get your hands off her." He stepped closer, but stayed out of arm's reach.

Mel tried again to force her way past, but the guards grabbed her by her upper arms and held her. She growled, and her eyes filled with tears.

John stepped toward the nearest guard, grabbed his free hand, and wrenched the guard's arm behind his back as he took a second step. The guard released his grip on Mel. John growled into the man's ear from inches away, "Tell your buddy to let my daughter go, or I will dislocate your shoulder." The soldier hesitated and John pulled up on his arm just enough to draw a sharp, pained breath from him.

The corporal and the two guards from the far door approached but stayed out of reach. "Sergeant," the corporal said, "there are seven of us. What do you think is going to happen here?"

"For starters, you're going to let my daughter go," John

said. "Then you're going to tell us where you've taken her husband."

"Fine." The corporal nodded to the other soldier, who released Mel and stepped back to block the door. "Now, let's be clear—access to the quarantine facility is restricted. We cannot allow you to enter."

Mel struggled to maintain her composure as waves of frustration and anger played across her face.

"Mel," John said, "please."

She glared at him, but after a moment's hesitation, took a half-step back.

"Quarantine?" John asked the corporal.

"We've taken Mr. Barber for additional testing and evaluation by our medical staff, and we will provide him whatever treatment is necessary." John opened his mouth, but the corporal held up a gloved hand to stop him before he could speak. "I am not authorized, nor do I have the time to go into any more detail. There are others behind you, awaiting evaluation and processing. Please Sergeant, release PFC Barnes and follow me to processing, or we will escort you there without your cooperation. Any further questions or concerns you have, you can take up with your building representative."

*Mel will be pissed, but what choice do we have, really?* John unwound himself from the private's pinned arm, stepped back, and patted the soldier's shoulder. "Sorry, Private. No hard feelings, I hope."

The private shook the feeling back into his hand, and though it was difficult to see through the visor, John felt fairly certain the young man's glare would've melted stone. Nevertheless, he quietly stepped back to his place near the door.

*Not sure I'd have played it that cool when I was a private.*

In the next room, the corporal pulled full-face gas masks from a nearly empty rack and handed them to John and Mel. Big red and black "Warning" signs flanked the only other door and promised illness or death to anyone who passed through without proper protective gear.

"Decon?" John took the mask and adjusted its straps, then helped Mel with hers.

"You could call it that," the corporal replied. "I always thought this was a war-time CBRN protocol, but the cadre told us to set it up, so we set it up."

"Better safe than sorry," John said, then put on and cleared his own mask.

"Something like that." The corporal checked the fit on Mel's mask and made minor adjustments. "Inhale." He covered the front of her mask with his hand. "And exhale." He moved his hands to cover the filters on either side. "Now, try to inhale again, pretty hard. Okay, good. Does that feel okay?"

Mel just nodded. It'd been twenty years since John had showed her how to don and clear a mask, back when she was a hyper-curious little girl and she and Mary still lived on base. Honestly, he was surprised he still remembered. *But that's why they drilled it into our heads in Basic... and every other damn chance they got.*

"I can check you too, if you want," the corporal said, "but it looks like you know what you're doing already."

"I'm good," John said. "Let's just get on with it."

The corporal led them through the plastic-strip door which turned out to be another short airlock, then through a series of small two-by-two meter rooms filled with mists of varying density and color. They exited the fourth of these rooms via airlock into a short tunnel like the one at the outer entrance where fans sucked air up through the grated floor past them. They walked down and exited the tunnel by airlock into yet another plastic-walled room where a private and a PFC, dressed in standard issue fatigues, took their masks and handed them paper towelettes that felt cold and smelled like lemons and chemicals. The privates immediately cleaned and disinfected the masks to ready them for the next group.

"Alright, you two should be as clean as you've ever been—from a contaminant perspective, at any rate," the corporal said, "but you need to wipe your face and hair thoroughly with those towels, especially where the masks covered, and I recommend you change out of your clothes as soon as you get settled, and have them reclaimed." He waited for them to finish, then opened the next door. "Now, let's step outside," he said, and waited for them to walk through.

They emerged into an immense cave awash in artificial light. The cave walls disappeared into near perfect darkness, fifteen meters or more above them. It might have started as a natural cave, but the bare rock walls bore the marks left by equipment used to smooth out and expand it. From near where they stood, two rows of enormous floor-to-ceiling pillars ran toward the rear of the cave as far as John could see.

More incredible, however, were the two plain concrete structures that nestled against either wall. Their sheer faces had few distinguishing marks. The building across from them stood two or three stories tall, and featured a double-door with simple lettering carved into the facade above that John couldn't quite make out.

The building behind them was equally plain, and though about a third of it was only a single story, the rest reached as high as the cave's ceiling. Windows on its three upper floors faced the rear of the cave. The door they'd just exited and the plastic maze they'd come from nuzzled up against the building like a translucent tent city that glowed with internal light. Nearby, a door into the single-story section had *INFIRMARY* carved into the concrete above it. About two-thirds of the way down, a second door stood under the inscription: *675TH MISSION SUPPORT GROUP.*

The light dimmed, and John and Mel turned to realize that the massive doors at the cave's entrance had slowly begun to close. Mel stepped closer and gripped his arm in both hands as the last sliver of natural light disappeared. John waited for the sound of bolts, gears, and locks to come as the doors shut and were secured. Next to him, Mel held her breath.

The silence was broken, not by mechanical sounds, but by the very human sound of the soldier who jogged toward them.

"Ah, here's the private," the corporal said. "He'll give you the nickel tour and show you to your bunks." As soon as the private reached them, the corporal handed his copy of the processing form over and said, "Three. We held one for evaluation." To John and Mel he said, "good luck," then turned on his heel and walked back through the door.

The private caught his breath as he glanced at the form, then started back the way he'd come and motioned for them to follow. "This way, please," he said between breaths.

John fell into step after him, and Mel stammered and scrambled to catch up.

"Welcome to the Northern California Emergency Sequestration Facility," the private began in a monotone, "this facility was designed to house and provide for survivors of a natural or geo-political catastrophe. To the left is our headquarters, which includes our administrative offices, meeting and training rooms, gym and lockers, as well as the command, communications, and medical facilities." He turned slightly as he walked and indicated the opposite building. "Across the way here is the physical services building..."

They had come close enough to the building to make out the inscription over the door. The top of two lines read: *PHYS-ICAL SERVICES*, and the second, in smaller letters, read: *COMPANY MESS.*

John's stomach growled loudly. "Speaking of the mess hall," he said, "any chance there's food where we're going? We haven't had a lick since dinner last night before all hell broke loose."

"I'll point out the civilian's dining hall on the way to your room. You're welcome to visit any time once you've settled in."

"Private, I'm starving, if we don't stop, I'm liable to eat you before we **get** to our room."

"Sorry sir, there are more than a hundred people still being processed, and only five of us assigned to this escort detail, so I need to get you to your room and come back for the next group."

"John, I'm about to pass out," Mel said. "I'm exhausted. My feet are killing me. And I'm worried about the baby. I'm hungry, but I need to rest. Right now, I need rest more than I need food."

John gritted his teeth. "Okay, but as soon as we're in the room, I'll come back and get us something."

Ten meters ahead, a chain-link fence spanned the width of the cave. They approached a gate with soldiers posted on either side, who opened and closed it behind them.

About ninety meters past the fence, a building sat in the middle of the cave. Beyond and just visible above it, two larger buildings stood on either side of the cave, their front corners part of two of the enormous pillars and their backs formed by the cave walls.

They walked around the smaller building and emerged in a throng of people. Hundreds milled about in the space between the two larger buildings and eight identical, previously hidden buildings that lined both sides of the cave and formed a long avenue. Light from the ceiling illuminated everything in large, soft pools. Only the rough-hewn rock walls reminded them where they were.

"Whoa," Mel said.

"Heard of places like this before," John said, "Cheyenne Mountain, Weather Mountain, the Greenbrier. But this is beyond anything I imagined."

They passed in front of the small building and the private pointed to the entrance. "This is the dining hall. Go through those doors and you'll find the cafeteria on the left and the dining area on the right. The residential buildings also have their own common dining rooms."

They crossed the busy avenue and navigated the sea of refugees. Trauma and loss etched every face.

"And here's your building," the private said.

They approached the first of the large buildings on the right side of the avenue. A large "2" was carved into the facade at the top left corner of the building.

"Building 2," he said, and consulted the form, "Room 412."

They entered through the front door at the building's center, into a small foyer furnished with benches and potted plants. *Probably fake.* The rear of the foyer opened onto a long hallway that appeared to run the length of the building. Directly across the hall from the foyer was an open stairwell. The private paused here.

"The building dining room, lounge, and a compositor facility are to the left," he said. "First floor restroom and bathing facilities are to the right—each floor has their own. Residential living units are all at the front of the building, while the community areas are at the back. There are no elevators, so the first floor is reserved for those with accessibility require-ments. Global datanet access is available throughout the cave if you have your own device, or you can use the hard-wired console in your room. Compositors in each building are freely available to use and, at the moment, unlimited—you may pull whatever items you need from the facility's exhaustive database."

The private led them up the stairs to the fourth floor, where a door opened onto a hallway nearly identical to the first.

"Your room's down this way." He led them down the hall to the right.

Room 412 sat at the end of the hall. The private unlocked and opened the door, then stepped out of the way so John and Mel could enter.

The small room featured a kitchenette set into the left wall, and a small dining table sat within the kitchenette's tiled floor. A seating area took up the rest of the room. Windows on the far wall afforded a view of Building One across the avenue. There were two doors along the right wall on the other side of the seating area.

"Beds?" Mel asked as she pulled a chair out from the table and sat down.

"Over here." The private walked past the chairs and sofa to one of the two doors. He opened the door, and a small, plain dresser was just visible, with a mirror hung over it. He walked to the second door and opened it, and revealed the corner of a very simple platform bed covered with a gray blanket. "There are unisex clothes in multiple sizes in the dressers. Keep what fits and return the rest. All textiles are organically rendered into and from raw materials. If something is soiled or worn, simply place it in the reclamation service." He pressed a panel in the wall between the two bedrooms, which opened to reveal an empty cabinet. "If you also press this button," he pointed to a round green button inside the cabinet, "we will replace your items in a few hours. Unfortunately, we can't launder or replace your civilian clothes. When you have them reclaimed, we will issue you new items according to your preferences. You can update your clothing or linen preferences or order new items via the console in your kitchen table."

Mel crossed her arms on the table and crumpled, facedown onto them.

The private crossed back to the kitchenette and picked a brochure up off the counter. "This has more information on clothing, meals, waste handling and reclamation, water and energy conservation, and other things you'll need to know." He opened a drawer. "Four copies of your room key are in this drawer. We'll post news and events on a bulletin board in the communal area downstairs, and to your console, and your building captain will be available to handle any concerns. We're here to keep you safe and alive until the doors re-open, so the rules are pretty simple: don't hurt yourself or someone else, don't waste shared resources, and don't make it harder for us to do our jobs. Any questions before I go?"

"Thank you private, I think we're good," John said.

"Sleep," Mel said into the table. "Food."

"Welcome to the Ark," the private said and slipped out the door.

———

JOHN TRIED to talk to Mel, but she was out. He helped her up and to one of the twin beds in the front bedroom, and covered her with the blanket from the room's other bed. Then he went back and systematically looked through the kitchenette's cabinets, and the small fridge and pantry. His search yielded a bounty of composited utensils, dishes, and glasses; cloth towels and napkins; an unopened case of MREs; and a single brown paperboard box labeled "dry cereal" in plain black type. *Hm. Maybe if we get really desperate.*

John washed his face and hands in the sink and dried them on one of the towels. He needed a shower, but he needed food more, so he pocketed a room key and slipped out the door.

He retraced their path through the building and back out onto the crowded avenue, and made his way toward the dining hall. He weaved between clusters of people dressed either in their ratty civilian clothes or the new uniformly gray shelter-issued outfits that looked somewhere between sweats and hospital scrubs.

"Hey, John!"

He turned toward the call, but didn't see any familiar faces. He'd started to turn back toward the cafeteria when a man in gray limped out on a crutch from behind a small, quiet group centered on a few monks. "John!" the man called to him and waved.

He seemed familiar, but it took John a moment to recognize Tom, the injured man they'd met on the mountain only a few hours ago. He'd cleaned up and dressed in fresh clothes, but his face was haggard and drawn, and his smile hardly penetrated his obvious exhaustion.

"Oh, hey Tom," John replied. "If you don't mind my saying so, you look like shit. Have you gotten any sleep?"

"Not yet," he said. "I've been bouncing around here and there since we got set up, same as most, it seems. I'd just rather be up and about, talking to people. The docs checked out my leg and replaced my splint, and gave me this getup to replace my clothes. Now I look like one of the chosen."

John chuckled but didn't reply, and Tom's tone grew more serious. "I saw what happened to you guys outside, and I just wanted to say I'm sorry if I got you nabbed. I told that soldier that Danny needed medical attention. I had no idea he'd have you guys dragged off like that."

"I appreciate it, Tom, but honestly, I don't think it would have gone any different. There or up at one of those tables, the state Daniel was in, they'd have hauled us off either way." They walked toward the dining hall, and John recounted for Tom most of what had happened since they'd separated at the entrance.

Tom whistled. "This is some crazy shit! What the fuck is going on here?"

"I wish I knew, son."

They walked through the doors into the packed cafeteria. In the common lounge area, people huddled around in front of a large screen that displayed what appeared to be a grid of live feeds from reporters outside the cave. Some feeds randomly went black or devolved into digital noise. Most of those gathered sat in mesmerized silence, or collapsed into tears or hysterics. John paused, transfixed, as feeds from all over the world cycled through the grid. Slowly, he realized that in all that jumble, there were no reports from Mars.

He and Tom moved on and joined the cafeteria line, which moved briskly.

Tom leaned in and whispered. "I've heard they quarantined hundreds during processing. A lady in my building said there've already been two groups of MP's through there hauling people off to who knows where."

The guy ahead of them looked back over his shoulder as the line inched forward. "They took the guy from next door to me. We was just standing there in the hall and here they come. Seems like somebody heard the dude sneeze, reported him, and next thing we know they's there and dragged him away."

Tom nearly shouted, "Holy shit!"

"Yeah," the guy leaned closer and whispered so the soldier behind the counter couldn't hear. "I hear the buildin' captains are reportin' the littlest shit—turning people in for havin' a cold, gettin' in fights, sayin' crazy shit, stuff like that." He reached the counter and took a tray.

Tom motioned for John to go ahead, "I've eaten."

John picked up a tray and two plates.

"One per person," the soldier said.

"Specialist, my daughter is back in our room asleep and hasn't eaten in twelve hours. I need to take her something."

"One plate."

"Y'know what," Tom said, "I am hungry." He picked up a

tray and took the extra plate from John, but kept his eyes on the soldier.

The soldier hesitated, then sighed. "Keep the line moving."

They proceeded down the line, and John pointed out things Mel would like while he filled his own plate. At the end of the line, with both plates full, John thanked Tom. "Mel will appreciate it when she wakes up."

"No problem," Tom said. "I'm glad to help, especially after all that's happened."

Tom struggled a bit between the crutch and the tray, so John took the second plate from him and put the extra tray in the collection area near the door.

They exited the building into a commotion. Several meters away, four soldiers carried something through the crowd. Where the crowd parted to let them through there was quiet, but where John and Tom stood on the outskirts, rumors and speculation burbled among a jumble of voices.

"… nasty fight in building three…"

"… those thugs beat up an old guy and killed him…"

"… they'll be cracking down now, heard that was one of theirs…"

"… girl hung herself in building five…"

The look in the soldiers' eyes and the way they moved told John well enough what was going on. He'd seen it too many times in the aftermath of battles across Afghanistan, Iraq, and Syria. A glimpse through the crowd confirmed that the soldiers carried a stretcher between them, the occupant draped in gray from head to toe.

Tom trembled, his face drawn and pale, and his eyes wet with tears. "I'll help you get this to your room," he stammered, "if that's alright."

"Of course, son," John said, "of course."

## NEW WORLD

Mel woke up in bed, and it felt like the baby had lodged its feet under her ribs. She gripped the covers in the dark, unfamiliar room as a wave of vertigo passed. Indistinct sounds from beyond the door slowly registered as John's voice. She swung her legs over the side of the bed and put her feet on the floor.

As she walked to the door, a second voice joined John's. *Danny!* She burst through the door, but the sight of the stranger in the chair opposite John stopped her cold and startled her the rest of the way awake.

"Oh," John said. "Good morning, sleepyhead."

Mel stood in the doorway and stared. Despite the monochrome gray outfit, the stranger's face seemed somewhat familiar.

"You remember Tom?" John asked. "We met him and Nolan on the way here."

She clenched her fist and scowled. *I remember he turned Danny in.* "You were dirtier then," Mel said. "If somewhat better dressed."

"Sweetie," John said, "Tom brought you some food." He pointed his thumb toward the little fridge.

"Ugh, thanks." *Don't think you can buy my forgiveness with food.* Mel skirted the chairs on her way to the fridge. "How long've I been out? I could eat a horse."

"Sorry, they were all out of horse," Tom said. "I think."

"Funny." Mel rummaged about the fridge.

"You've been asleep about four hours," John said.

"Four hours? What've you boys been up to?"

"This and that. Talking, mostly." John said. "Tom's buddy Nolan got tapped to work the quarantine."

Mel bolted from the fridge to Tom's chair, her hands stuffed with dinner rolls and sliced ham. She kneeled down and rested her elbows against the arm of his chair, and invaded his personal space with cold rolls. "Have you heard anything about Danny? Is he okay?"

Tom recoiled and stammered.

"Mel. Calm down," John said. "Tom hasn't been able to talk to Nolan yet."

"When you do," Mel said, "can you ask about Danny?"

"Sure?" Tom said. "He messaged me once when he had a free moment. Said they're super busy, but he didn't want me to worry. I'll ask him about Danny as soon as I can."

"Thank you." Mel stood and walked to the windows. She tore open a roll and stuffed it with ham. On the avenue below, people milled about between buildings and congregated in small groups. Most of them wore gray outfits like Tom's, while the rest still had on their own clothes. At least three people wandered the avenue with scraps of cardboard scrawled with the words "Repent" or "The End Is Here" in large dark letters. They shouted and waved their signs in the face of anyone who got close enough. In front of building one, someone had draped a table with gray bedsheets on which they'd written "Goverment," "SHEEP," and "Ginny Pigs," and littered it with what appeared to be some kind of pamphlets. *Crazy, but industrious.*

Several soldiers rounded the dining hall at a run and headed down the avenue. At the limit of the view afforded by the windows, a knot of people just off the avenue between buildings three and five shouted at others they'd surrounded. The crowd swayed and moved like it held something that wanted out. Fists and elbows flew as individuals, thrown against the circle, were shoved back toward the middle. The soldiers tried to break through the crowd, but were pushed out themselves. They drew their sticks and dove back in. People fell or fled, and the circle broke apart. The soldiers pushed or dragged four young men onto the avenue and toward the military compound. The rest they left to pick themselves up.

"What the hell is going on out there?" Mel asked.

"What do you mean?" John asked.

"MPs just broke up a nasty-looking fist fight."

"Hm. Not surprised," Tom said. "Lots of people out there are looking for explanations... or excuses. I had to get away from a couple of groups that were threatening to boil over because of some fundamental differences of opinion. Nobody really knows what's going on, but plenty of people think they do and think they know whose fault it is."

More MPs rounded the corner and headed into building three. "They are certainly busy," Mel said.

"Rumor is," John replied, "they're taking more and more people into quarantine, or just detaining them... nobody's quite sure."

Mel continued to eat her little sandwiches as the chaos played out in the avenue below. "But what can we do about it?" She asked, "If it's already this bad, what hope do we have for Danny?"

"I don't know," John said. "We need to figure out what's going on."

"There's some big meeting tonight," Tom said. "I think

they're planning one in each building. May be a good place to start."

"Good," John said. "We'll go to ours. In the meantime, try to get a message to Nolan and see if he can tell us anything. The brass is going to tell us what they think we want to hear, and it would help to get an unfiltered view of what's going on in there."

The heads of the soldiers posted by the gate were just visible above the dining hall roof. Beyond them, nestled up next to the Army building, the quarantine area glowed. Danny was there. *Alone.* Mel touched her belly. *We'll get you out of there. One way or another.*

MEL SIPPED on what was purportedly an English breakfast tea that somehow was both more pungent and less potent than anything from her previous experience of the type. Before today, she might have complained, returned to the refreshments table for another option, or simply set the cup down and forgotten it, but it seemed such minor disappointments would be part of the new normal for a while. As in the dark as they all were, it was clear they'd have many adjustments to make. Some would be easier than others.

Hot tea, for example, was something Mel had never really been interested in, and she imagined if it ever became truly unpalatable, she'd be perfectly happy with distilled water.

A few people huddled around monitors at the side of the room with their dinner plates, enthralled by breathless news reports from the surface. She'd learned to tune out the news media years ago after they'd all started featuring amateur field reporters with satellite-connected follow drones. *There's enough pain and drama every day without bringing more in intentionally.*

The war-zone reports in particular always reminded her of

the footage from reporters embedded with her dad's unit who'd been recording when they hit the IED. As a young girl, Mel had replayed the footage over and over while she struggled to make sense of his death.

These reports had the same frenzied earnestness, so now she sat, stirred her tea, and ignored the noise and chaos.

Frustration in the room was palpable, but it mostly centered on petty things like the drab gray everything, the bland food, and the claustrophobic nature of the cave. It would be pointless to bring up Danny's abduction in this environment, and an insult to put it on the same level as someone's distaste for rehydrated, cultured chicken protein.

Mel stirred while others speculated about the catastrophe that had driven them here, or lamented the family they'd left behind. The last time Mel had seen her mom, she'd absent-mindedly stirred a cup of tea while she filled Mel in on extended family drama and neighborhood gossip. Wisps of steam danced as she talked.

Had she found shelter? Was she somewhere safe now, with fresh gossip on her lips while a cup of tea cooled on a table in front of her? *What was it she kept saying after Dad died?*

*"When times are tough, you focus on what's ahead. Maybe next week, maybe tomorrow, maybe even the next five minutes. Whatever it takes. Tears will come, there's no stopping 'em, but the world won't end as much as you might want it to. You do that and when the tough times end, you'll be a little bit stronger."*

She'd taught Mel to deal with what was in front of her, to face each day on its own terms. But Danny was in here and Mel needed to see him, to hold him, to know he was okay— then they could stop, take stock, and deal with the next day, together.

She sipped her tea as John recounted their climb over the

mountain for a few interested ears, his animated story peppered with anecdotes from his time in Afghanistan and Iraq in the late 2010s. Usually Mel enjoyed his penchant for story-telling, but she was too preoccupied to engage with him today.

The door opened, and a lieutenant walked in, cap in hand, her regulation hair in a regulation bun, followed by a civilian puffed up with pomp and authority.

They walked to the refreshments table—a paltry affair that featured air pots filled with passable tea and less passable coffee, creamer and sweetener of unknown origin, gray composited cups, and plain crackers. The civilian picked up the sugar spoon and rapped it on the table several times until conversations died down.

"Hello everyone," he said. "Thank you for coming. For those of you who've not yet met me, I'm Robert Gillet, your building captain. This is Lieutenant Hasty from the 675th, who is here to share some news and answer your questions. Please give her your full attention."

"Thank you, Mr. Gillet." Lt. Hasty took a few steps forward. "First, I'm sure you're all wondering what's happened, and unfortunately, I have to tell you we still don't know much. All I can say with certainty is that there was a major astronomical event last night that resulted in earth-quakes, volcanic eruptions, tsunami, flooding, and unparalleled weather events across the globe, as well as the complete destruction of the moon and our orbital colonies. We don't yet understand the full impact of this event, but sensors outside the cave show the air is choked with smoke and ash, and, as you've doubtless seen from the reports, this is true almost everywhere. We estimate that within a week, maybe two, maybe less, the surface will be completely inhospitable. Little hope remains for anyone still out there."

Mel's throat tightened, and tears flooded her eyes. She thought of her mother's house—her coyote brush and mums weighed down under a blanket of ash, their brilliant colors washed gray and black.

"The loss of life is incalculable," the lieutenant continued, "but if all nine of the known shelters like this one are operational and fully populated, the total surviving human population living within them will be around 25,000."

A very pregnant woman choked back a sob and ran from the room, which bubbled with questions and conversations.

How long had she and Danny talked about having a baby —about whether they were mature enough, or settled enough, or responsible enough to bring another life into the world? *That world.* Mel froze. *Oh my god.* She'd been so focused on Danny, she hadn't considered what all this meant for the baby. *To bring a baby into this world, and without Danny… a nightmare within a nightmare.*

"Our communications officers have been working around the clock," the lieutenant continued, "to establish communications with those other facilities, but apart from freelance news reports, we've had no direct contact with the outside since the event."

John sat up straighter next to Mel and asked, "What about the Mars colony?" The lieutenant chewed on a response, so John continued. "You mentioned the orbital and lunar colonies, but not Mars. Have you attempted to contact the Martian colonists?"

"I… don't have access to that information, currently," she replied. "The comms officers are pursuing every possibility, but Mars didn't appear in my summary briefing for this meeting. I'll make sure to ask when I get back to HQ."

On the other side of the room, a lady asked, "So, what the hell happened out there?"

"Like I said, we don't exactly know. The last report we received was of a massive, dark, rapidly approaching object. Prevailing credible theories suggest a black hole, moving too fast for advance detection." The lieutenant shifted on her feet, then held up her hands. "Which brings me to my next topic."

"This facility was originally built in the late 1960s in anticipation of a global nuclear event. Our air is heavily filtered. We have food and other supplies to last two thousand people up to five years. With over twenty-five hundred of us here, we're a bit overcrowded, but with careful rationing, what we have should still last nearly that long. If we determine we won't be able to re-open the doors before our supplies run out, we will enact long-term occupation protocols." She continued, "In the meantime, our aquaponics facility will supplement our food supply and help filter our water and air. We are strategically located with access to nearby surface and underground lakes, which we will harvest additional water from if it becomes necessary." The lieutenant shifted her weight from foot to foot. "The 675th Mission Support Group has occupied and operated this facility since its inception for almost 85 years, and our primary mission has always been the protection and preservation of our country, and our species, at any cost."

Lt. Hasty stepped back and glanced at the captain. "To do that, we need your trust and cooperation. It is vitally important for you all to take care of each other, to be mindful of our resources, and ultimately, to settle in and make this work. Along with your civilian building captains, we've assigned each building a trained counselor from our staff, and I encourage all of you to schedule a session as soon as possible, whether or not you feel the need. Your building captains will be our liaison to you, and, along with our counselors, will help ensure that we are all doing everything we can to make our time here pass as quickly and uneventfully as possible."

"That all sounds great," Mel stood in front of her seat, "but I think I speak for a lot of people here who want to know what the hell is going on with the quarantine and what you're doing with the people you're abducting."

John reached up and touched her forearm gently.

"We want answers," she continued, "and we want our family back."

"Ma'am, the quarantine is for your protect…"

"Bullshit!" Mel shouted. "My husband had a cold and was worn out from crossing a mountain in the middle of the night, and you took him! I've gotten no word from him or about him since this morning!"

"Ma'am, if you could just calm down, please."

"No, I'm not going to fucking calm down! I want to know how my husband is!"

The lieutenant gestured, and soldiers entered the room.

"Mel…" John said in a quiet growl as the MPs crossed the room toward her.

"I want to know when my husband is being released! I want assurances that he's being taken care of. I want assurances that he's even still alive! We've all heard the rumors: that you're withholding treatment, that you're letting people die in there! How can we trust you when you won't even let us talk to them! When will these people get to see their friends and family again, and when do we get to feel safe here!"

The soldiers came down their row from either side, and people scrambled to get out of the way.

"I want answers! I want to see my husband!" Mel shouted.

The soldier in front of her grabbed her forearm and yanked her down the row toward the aisle.

John exploded toward the soldier who had approached from the other direction and knocked him to the floor. Blood ran from the soldier's nose. John maneuvered around Mel and shouted, "Get your hands off her!" He attacked the soldier who held Mel, and she fell back into an empty chair. People rallied around her to make sure she was okay, and she lost sight of what was happening.

John shouted, "Son, you do not manhandle a pregnant lady like that!"

Mel struggled to sit up as the commotion continued. Another soldier grabbed John from behind and in a flash had his baton between John's legs and had lifted him up onto his toes and perilously off-balance.

"John, no!"

The soldier steered John to the door and out of the room.

The lieutenant glared at Robert. "Deal with this," she said, and stormed out.

"Bring him back!" Mel yelled as the building captain raised his hands to restore order.

---

# DAY TWO

---

**New York City**

*4pm, 24 August 2048*

The intersection at Fifth and Broadway—normally awash
in light and noise—is empty and quiet. Filtered light from the overcast sky
throws weak shadows at odd angles.

Washed out cars line the streets, smashed together or overturned, and
mingled with debris and bodies left by receding floodwaters and the rubble
from collapsed or damaged buildings. The Flatiron stands, but her tattered
facade lies scattered on the ground.

Madison Square Park is alive with the chatter of birds and squirrels
that echoes through the concrete chasms and off the dense, encroaching
clouds.

A gunshot rings out in the distance. Somewhere nearby, metal clangs
and glass shatters, frightening the animals into momentary silence.

A woman, unkempt and dirty, cautiously steps over the broken glass
and shattered terra-cotta that litters the ground. Draped with a blanket
against the unseasonable chill, she carries her scavenged spoils wrapped in
one of its corners.

In the park, something crashes to the ground, driving birds to flight, and she cranes her neck to find the sound's source, taking a tentative step in its direction. Then her shoulders drop, her face darkens, and she glances away from the park down Broadway. She moves, and a moment later disappears west up 22nd Street.

# IN FOR A FIGHT

Mel strode down the brightly lit hallway. In the building's common areas, as in the cave itself, the lighting cycled between full sun and half-moon in an artificial mockery of the outside world. It was never truly dark except in her windowless bedroom. The cycle was meant to add a sense of order and routine, but the survivors didn't care.

It was also never quiet, because someone was always awake and the avenue outside crawled with humanity. Inside every room Mel passed, people screamed, sobbed, fought, or fucked. She ignored it all.

A door ahead of her slammed open and two men tumbled out. They pummeled each other with fists, knees, and elbows, and Mel stepped around them carefully. The pregnant woman who'd run from yesterday's meeting sat at the kitchen table beyond the open door, her eyes red and face wet with tears.

*Everything's falling apart, Danny.*

The girl looked at her and her face became Mel's face. Overcome by vertigo, Mel stumbled. She closed her eyes, clenched her jaw, and moved on.

*I need you here.*

As she neared the stairwell, the door burst open and four MPs streamed through. The first three carried a stretcher past her and past the men who wrestled on the ground, while the fourth drew his baton and shouted at them. "Break it up!"

One flailed and kicked the soldier's shin, and the MP brought his stick down hard on the man's back, then grabbed his hand, wrenched his arm behind his back, and pressed him down to the floor. With barely a look, he put his boot on the other man's neck. "Break it up, or I'll break your arm."

Mel continued through the stairwell door—she didn't want to know which door the stretcher entered. Like every other horrible thing that had happened since they got here, talk of the latest suicide would be inescapable. They'd say *he seemed like he had it together*, or *oh, I saw her a few hours ago looking like a ghost*. The mumbled conversations and all the death made her want to puke.

*Is what's left even worth living for? Could I do it? What would they say about me?* She descended steps that existed in some other world. *How?* The windows didn't open. The shower curtain rod was too weak. *Knife?* She slid her hand down the handrail—*belt over the banister?* Whoever discovered her would scream—*they always screamed*. The MPs would take her down. Someone would have to tell John. *Someone would have to tell Danny. Someone would have to tell Danny about the baby.*

Tears welled. She stumbled on the second floor landing as a vision of Danny in a hospital bed, wracked with grief, careened through her head. Grief on top of grief on top of grief. *Where would it end?*

*Why are they keeping him from me?*

She needed to see him. To hold him. Needed him with her. She needed to make sure he was okay.

At the bottom of the stairs, she stepped out into the hallway and headed toward the counselor's office.

*Once Danny's okay, once he's here, once he's safe, then we can deal with everything else. Right now, I'm going to fix this.*

She would make someone fix it or she would raise some serious hell until they did.

---

MEL OPENED the door and entered. Her body was hard, cold marble, but her head and her heart were fire.

"Come in, Mrs. Barber, please. Sit down." The officer—a Captain if Mel's fuzzy memory of rank insignia was right—gestured toward the chair across from his desk, which was littered with folders and files. One file sat open in front of him, next to a legal pad.

Mel sat poised on the edge of the chair, back straight and gaze fixed. *Average, if a bit scrawny for a Captain. He doesn't have a prayer.*

"I want my husband released." Her voice was steel.

"Your husband is…" he glanced at the file, "in quarantine."

"Yes, and I want him released."

"I'm afraid I don't have that kind of authority."

"You're part of the medical staff."

"Yes."

Her words came out dark and measured, "Then you find someone who has the authority, and release my husband."

"You're worried about him."

"Of course I'm worried about him," she said. "You *know* what's going on."

"I'm aware of rumors about the quarantine."

"Rumors! If they're just rumors, why haven't you released anyone? Why won't you let us talk to them? Rumors!" She tried to rein herself back in. "We may not know exactly what's happening inside the quarantine, but we can damned well see what's going on out here! Your soldiers are bullies and thugs! We've all already lost everything. Things are bad enough without you making them worse."

"You're having trouble dealing with your grief."

Mel seethed. "You think this is grief talking, you shit-heel? You think you know grief?" She stood and pounded the table. "You have taken my husband from me, you've taken everything I had and left me nothing." She leaned in, her words practically a growl, "You tell your CO, *we know*. We see what's happening. He will fix this, now, and give me my husband back, or I will hold **you** responsible, and I will make **you** pay. You **all** will pay for it, for all of it."

She straightened and turned toward the door. Her body shivered from the rush of adrenaline. She stepped through the door and slammed it shut behind her.

---

MEL SET the little table in her room with food she and Tom had brought up from the cafeteria. It wasn't exactly four-star, but it beat the dehydrated cultured meat and packaged meals that filled the cupboards. She pulled napkins and flatware from the drawers while Tom filled cups with water.

He'd come to visit with John, but when she'd told him about how they'd taken John away, Tom had offered to stay and keep her company. Mel suspected that his guilt over Danny motivated his concern, and though grudges were a particular strength of hers, she appreciated his attempt to make amends. She adjusted the napkin and utensils next to her plate.

"Something on your mind?" Tom asked.

"Honestly? I half expected to have been hauled off before now," Mel said. "Guess the counselor didn't find an angry pregnant woman all that intimidating."

"I'd bet he's getting a hundred different variations of that today. The counselor in my building was about the same. Said he had no insight or input into the quarantine, but that we should be patient and let things work themselves out."

"Right," Mel said. "While the goon squads are abducting people and everyone we talk to is either patronizing or combative, we're supposed to trust and be patient. If they would just let us talk to them!"

"I thought for sure Nolan would have at least messaged me by now," Tom said. "They must have things really locked down in there."

"And things out here are getting worse," Mel said. "Groups are coming together, splintering, or isolating themselves. We've got to do something else—something more than just complaining and asking questions that no one with any authority wants asked." Mel pushed vegetables around her plate and poked at the steaming chicken.

The survivors continued to grow untethered and unhinged. A prayer vigil blocked half the avenue, while a group of ascetics tried to burn their clothes between two of the buildings. There were rumors that a suicide cult had barricaded themselves in building four, and that hedonists engaged in a perpetual orgy had taken over the entire third floor of building three. Arguments, fistfights, and all-out brawls drew the soldiers' swift and increasingly frustrated, violent response.

"A petition?" Tom asked. "We could send it to every building, get signatures, and show them it's not just a handful of malcontents."

"A petition?" Mel smirked. "An assault! We'll dismantle our furniture for weapons. They'll never see us coming!" She flourished with her knife in the air.

"Every one of them is armed," Tom said. "We wouldn't stand a chance. If they started shooting, the cave would be a charnel house."

Mel's smile disappeared. "The whole world is a charnel house. What've we got left to lose?"

"People are terrified and broken," Tom said, "but you'll never convince enough of them to take that risk."

Mel ran her thumbs over the handles of her knife and fork. "It was just a stupid joke." The utensils' texture and density was somewhere between ceramic and the biopolymers such things were more commonly made of in the world outside the cave. She laid them back on her plate, her food mostly uneaten. "A… protest then. A demonstration," she said.

"A protest," Tom repeated, "would be less risky, but visible, depending on how big it is."

Mel picked up her utensils, cut a bite of chicken, and ate. The meat was tender and juicy, but flavorless. "I'd still rather just go knock their heads together," she said. "But these people need something. All we have now is loss and fear, and if it keeps going the way it's going, the Army will crack down and we'll be living under a police state. It feels like we're almost there already. The people need somewhere to redirect their energy, something to give them hope. Maybe a protest can give them that."

If Danny were here, and John, she might be content to sit in their rooms and talk about old times, about what had happened, about what was going on around them, and about what the future might look like. Under the US Army's olive drab wing, she'd learned that change is life and that you either adapt and move on or you fall out and let life kick your ass. She didn't know if she could adapt to this. *Not without Danny.*

She knew she couldn't sit here and blindly trust he was okay and that things would work out. Before, she'd believed that causes were for people with nothing better to do—but now, for her, there *was* nothing. She had to save Danny, or give in and die.

"We can't let them do this, right?" she wiped a tear from

her cheek. John was her mentor, her stand-in father, her rock. He would've known what to do.

"The Army may be overwhelmed, but that's no excuse for what they're doing," Tom said. "They have to be reigned in."

"I don't think they're going to just release everyone because we ask nicely."

"There are nearly three-thousand of us," Tom said, "so, numbers-wise, we have the advantage. We've just got to hope that enough others are as fed up as we are and want to do something. Then, maybe, we won't have to ask *so* nicely."

"There's another meeting in the lounge tomorrow," Mel said. "That's probably as good a place to start as any."

---

# DAY THREE

## Louisville

---

*9am, 25 August 2048*

THE BELLE OF LOUISVILLE RESTS PRECARIOUSLY HALFWAY UP THE *remains of an empty exit ramp, the maw of the whale-shaped arena looming nearby. Covered by a fine layer of gray-black ash, her broken paddle-wheel turns listlessly in the wind. The entire waterfront is coated with brown river mud and debris washed up by massive waves that traveled up the Mississippi, surmounted the locks, and destroyed the dams in their forceful passage. The air, choked with ash and dust, smells of sulfur and decay. Louisville's older buildings lay disheveled, most erect but denuded, some reduced entirely to rubble in the streets.*

*There is little sound or movement beyond the wind and water and the packs of dogs roving the empty streets. Heavy gray smoke wafts from the open balcony door of a nearby building, where firelight flickers through sheer curtains hung in river-facing windows.*

# THE FRYING PAN

IF HIS YEARS IN THE MILITARY HAD TAUGHT JOHN ONE THING, IT was how to talk to the brass. As a civilian, he didn't cotton to the perpetuation of stereotypes—people and personalities were as diverse as fingerprints, if you bothered to delve below the surface. And John loved to delve. The military, however, was a different beast. The military life had a peculiar draw, and by John's reckoning, you could count on a handful of distinct personality types to join up. Army officers expressed a unique intersection of those types, with each advance in rank attended by its own quirks.

The 22-year-old butterbar next to him was a prime example. A young officer was eager for validation, so John had fed his ego while he shared a retired sergeant's advice on how to earn the respect of his NCOs and the other enlisted men and women under him. John's status as a veteran gave him leeway he wouldn't have otherwise had and, unlike out in the civilian world, he had no reservations here about using it to his advantage.

So John had talked his way into the lieutenant's good graces and out of the rooms they'd kept him and the other relatively stable, non-violent detainees in. These rooms were across the hall from the MP station in a suite of vacant offices, outfitted with cots and a shared lavatory. They locked up the violent, unstable ones in the stockade at the back of the MP station.

The lieutenant led him through a series of doors, stairways, and hallways up to the Colonel's office in the far corner on the third floor. It had taken some work, but in the end the officer believed it was his own idea. The lieutenant rapped on the door, then opened it and entered.

"Colonel," he said. "Lieutenant Harris, sir. I have one of the detainees here. A Sergeant Hoffstead, sir."

"Retired," John added.

Colonel Springer paced behind his desk somewhat unsteadily, his gaze fixed on the clipboard he carried. He seemed young for his rank and appeared to have gotten little sleep recently.

"Sergeant Hoffstead believes he can help us, sir. I thought you might like to talk to him."

"At ease, Sergeant..."

Since John had neither stood at attention nor saluted, there was no doubt as to the Colonel's distracted state of mind. John smirked. He'd often found officers' self-important preoccupation amusing, unit commanders' doubly so.

The colonel raised his eyes to look at John. "Ah, yes," he said, "you did say 'retired.' I thought I didn't recognize the name."

"No, sir. I hiked across the mountain with my daughter and her husband, and got here just before the doors closed."

"Well, we're certainly glad to have such resourceful and... experienced people such as yourself as part of our unfortunate little community, I'm sure." New furrows etched the colonel's brow as he glanced at his clipboard, then at his desk and its stacks of folders and half-finished paperwork. When he spoke again, his voice was harder. "I think my lieutenant here said something about you being a detainee? If you've been out there causing trouble for my soldiers, how exactly do you think you can help me, and why the hell should I listen? You're not part of my staff, and I am most obviously busy..." he waved his arm in the general direction of his desk, "so can you please tell me why you are standing on what would otherwise be a pleasantly empty spot on my carpet?"

John suppressed a chuckle. "Let me cut to the chase, Colonel—you've got a civilian problem. There's a boatload of scared, broken people out there, and instead of providing safety and comfort, your people are acting like they're running a prison camp. You put my son-in-law, Daniel, in quarantine for having a cold and, if the rumors are to be believed—and my experience here suggests they are—over two hundred others are being similarly held without good reason and without adequate care."

"All I'm hearing so far is a bunch of whining, Sergeant. What's your point?"

"My point, Colonel, is that the people out there aren't soldiers, they're not going to just accept what you tell them and do what you tell them. And if things keep going the way they're headed, you're either going to end up with a full-scale riot and lots of people will get hurt, or you really are going to have to turn this into a prison camp."

The colonel's face flushed—a mask of hard lines and narrow eyes. He was not accustomed to being questioned or accused of impropriety.

"First off," he said through clenched teeth, "you should know that we've been planning and training for something like this for years. The men and women under my command are hand-picked, down to the greenest E1—and not just for their military aptitude. What we are undertaking here is nothing less than a last-ditch effort to secure the future of the human race.

Protocols and plans are in place so that we may preserve and expand this Ark to take us through decades, if necessary." He dropped his clipboard on his desk. "But 'no plan survives contact with the enemy' as they say, and reality usually deviates from our expectations. As you may've noticed by the accommodations, they built this place to provide for a more… select group, not the rabble we ended up with. We're supposed to be supporting politicians, entrepreneurs, scientists, and their families. But we hadn't anticipated the precise event, or the directive to open our Ark to the public. It happened so fast. We implemented a contingency plan to pull people from their homes, their businesses, and schools." Some of the edge left his voice. "Our quarantine protocols were established—by brighter minds than mine—as the first line of defense for a vulnerable population. To accommodate the... relaxed selection criteria, we had to improvise, and, on the advice of our own medical staff and the civilian doctors we evacuated, we enacted an elevated version of the quarantine procedures, which is what you have seen. Our first... first priority is to assure the health and well-being of the survivors, and we will do that by whatever means are necessary. If they can't cope, can't adjust, then we have to do what we must, to protect everyone." The colonel fixed him with a glare. "We are an army of one hundred and fifty men and women, and all our enemies are either dead or locked in caves like this one. So we're left with only two enemies to fight: time, and disease. Given the situation, what else could we do?" he asked.

Men in the colonel's position don't ask that sort of question expecting an answer, so John simply waited.

The Colonel sighed. "The rumors you've heard are not entirely without merit. Some of those in quarantine are more than simply ill—a few have difficult-to-treat diseases or conditions that put an excessive burden on our limited resources." The colonel rounded the corner of his desk slowly and approached John. "We can't **afford** to maintain these individuals without hope of a cure, nor can we prolong or even tolerate the possibility of a deadly outbreak among such a confined, therefore vulnerable population." The colonel's tone and wide, unblinking stare sent shivers up John's spine. "Right now, our population is large enough to guarantee sustainable genetic diversity—which, if our time here might extend beyond a few decades, is something we **have to** consider. Even a minor epidemic could threaten that. Are you aware that since the doors closed we've had over fifty suicides, forty physical assaults, and at least five suspicious deaths? This is a psychological epidemic, and it requires an aggressive response. We will help those we can help, those who have a chance of safe re-integration, and we will make the rest as comfortable as possible until we determine an appropriate course of action. What we will not do is waste resources on those we can't save."

*He's unhinged.* John balled his fists and forced himself to breathe. He'd never had a problem telling the brass off when their shortsightedness threatened to put his platoon in unnecessary danger, but he'd never wanted to punch one quite this badly before. He gritted his teeth. "My father learned in Vietnam, as I'm sure you and I both learned in Iraq and Afghanistan, that *why you're fighting* isn't nearly as important as *how you win.*" He unclenched his fists. "The minute you compromise your principles, you cheapen your victory. Every moment we choose how we're to be remembered—as liberators or as killers, as protectors or as destroyers—one wrong choice can be difficult to undo, and harder to outlive." The colonel's face tensed, but John pushed ahead. "Make the right choice. If you want to save humanity, treat them like humans, not prisoners. Let these people—who have already lost everything—see their loved ones, even if only one at a time and under quarantine. They need to see—to know—that they're

OK. Otherwise the rumors will continue to spread, and you will lose the high ground."

"You come into my office and presume to lecture me!" The colonel stepped to within a foot of John and shouted down at him. "Where have you been the last ten years? Drying up in a retirement home? I've been here, *here*, preparing for this! You are in my world now, Sergeant, and you'd better not forget that."

John stood straight and still against the colonel's fury. "That is exactly why I'm here, sir. You've apparently been locked in your little world so long, you've forgotten what it's like outside of it." John gestured toward the window behind the colonel's desk. "Well, those people haven't. They've been stripped of their blue skies and their freedom, and they aren't used to taking orders or getting pushed around. You want this to function, you'd better get your head out of your ass so you can see what's going on around you. These people are broken, your people are broken. I'm broken." John calmed, but continued, "And I strongly suspect that you're broken as well. You want to save humanity, so save them! Don't destroy them."

"Harris!" the colonel screamed. "Get this fool out of my office!"

"I came here," John said, "to help you save them."

The lieutenant grabbed John's arm and pulled him toward the door.

"I've been between two worlds since I got out, Colonel," John said. "I'm a soldier. I'm a father. I'm one of you and I'm one of them. Let me help you!"

The lieutenant pulled John through the door.

"Make the right choice!" John shouted as the door closed.

THE LIEUTENANT FUMED and muttered under his breath as they descended the stairs to the second floor landing.

"Not your fault, son," John said. "Your CO is standing at the edge of a cliff and I pushed him, but he's got bigger things to worry about than an old man like me yelling at him."

The lieutenant grumbled.

"You were trying to help," John said. "And you can still help."

"Oh, I'm done helping you."

They reached the first floor, and John stopped just before the stairwell exit. "Now, look," he said, "right now, the biggest fear the people out there have is that their loved ones in quarantine are being neglected—that they're being left to die," John said.

"It's not true. The people in our medical facility and in quarantine are being well looked after."

"Okay, well, if that's true, it should be easy enough to prove," John said. "Take me in. Let me see that my son-in-law is okay. We can still help your soldiers and your CO by sharing an outsider's account of what's really going on in quarantine. When I'm released, I can help to ease their concerns, but first I need to see it for myself."

The door opened, and another lieutenant walked through. She gave a slight nod to John's companion as she stepped past them and headed up the steps.

"After what you pulled with the Colonel, I imagine it'll be some time before you see the outside of this building," the lieutenant said. "But I'll take you. Your son-in-law can tell you how well we're treating him. You'll see it's not at all like the rumors suggest."

He opened the door and gestured for John to follow, away from the detention area to a door in the middle of the next hallway marked simply "Medical Center."

The door opened into a large room with what appeared to

be a small seating area in the near corner, several doors around the periphery, and the middle dominated by a semicircle of desks with cabinets, shelves, and a bank of machines that flashed and beeped. A mix of people in scrubs and Army greens worked behind the desks, while a few patients in hospital gowns ambled around it. Except for the complete absence of windows and the high ratio of uniformed soldiers, John would have thought he'd stepped into an average small American hospital's in-patient wing.

All the doors had their function painted on them in big block letters: of the ones he could see, three were exam rooms, two were surgical suites, and one was marked "Emergency/Triage." There were four patient rooms, marked "B" through "E." He also saw one restroom and another room in the far corner, which was too far away to read.

The lieutenant walked up to the central station and nodded at the person seated behind the nearest desk. "What's your son's name?"

"Barber," John said. "Daniel Barber."

The nurse tapped on a slate for a moment, then handed it to the lieutenant who looked at it, scrolled through a screen or two, then handed it back. "This way," he said, and led John around the front of the desks. "You can see that we have a fully equipped, modern facility here. We have ten permanent beds, three exam rooms, two surgical bays, and a triage bay. Given what's happened, and the number of casualties we expected, the temporary structures and equipment were setup to provide additional beds and to function as a quarantine facility. We prioritize the most vulnerable patients and those who need closer monitoring or extra security into our primary rooms. Anyone who poses a significant infection risk goes to an isolation room in quarantine. Everyone else gets the first available room."

The lieutenant walked to the far left corner, to the set of

double-doors that John could now see was marked "Quarantine." The room they entered appeared to be nothing more than a storage and locker room, with a few rows of empty shelves in one corner, and lockers and benches in the other. Empty yellow hazmat suits hung between the lockers. Just inside the door, before the first locker, several suits hung together, each with red bands around the elbows. The lieutenant grabbed one of these and handed it to John. "Here, put this on," he said, then he walked to a locker with "HARRIS" stenciled above it in big block letters and took down the suit that hung next to it.

"What's the red for?" John asked.

"Guest suits," the lieutenant said. "So we can keep track of people who should have an escort."

"So, you're prepared to allow guests, you're just not?" John pulled the suit on over his clothes and the hood over his head while the lieutenant did the same, then he checked the baffles and zippers. *Long time since I had to put on anything like this.*

"Colonel's orders. He wants things to settle down a bit first." The lieutenant looked him over and nodded. "Alright then, let's go."

*Right.* The lieutenant's voice sounded clear inside the suit, though there was no obvious hardware or radio controls built into the hood or gloves. *Must have short-range auto-transceivers built in.*

They exited through another set of double-doors into a familiar room of plastic sheeting. It might have been the same room where they'd doffed their masks after decon the first day. *I was so exhausted… it's hard to say for sure.*

From here they went into the longer corridor with the gridded floor and giant fans that pulled air past them. The fans were going slowly when they stepped in, but quickly ramped up until the air whipped past them. The violent vibrations induced in the suit's fabric were almost too loud to bear.

They exited the airlock across from a small, unoccupied nurse's station with a single desk and mobile shelves stacked with linens and various supplies. The station sat at the intersection of perpendicular corridors that passed in front of the station to the left, and behind the station to the right. Light flooded the area from above the translucent ceilings. Small gray chips with engraved numbers hung over the entries to the rooms that lined the corridors.

"This way." The lieutenant led John left past the nurses' station and three sets of rooms, and around the corners of a short hallway to another corridor that was also lined with rooms. They stopped outside number seventeen. "Here he is," the lieutenant said.

Before they could enter, a loud, unpleasant alert tone pushed through layers of plastic, and a red light flashed over the entry to room twenty across the hall. Something metallic crashed loudly against the tile floor and the plastic corridor walls jerked strangely, then swayed gently as if in a light breeze.

The lieutenant sprinted toward the room with John on his heels. He flung aside the hanging door panels. A rolling cart and its contents littered the floor below a man who dangled by the cable he had tied between an overhead support and his now constricted neck. The man's bare, limp feet traced a slow path through mashed potatoes that had spilled from the cart onto the floor.

The lieutenant shouted for help while John ran into the room, wrapped his arms around the man, and lifted him up to put slack in the cord. "Come help me, damn it!" John yelled. "Get him down!"

The lieutenant ran into the room, pulled over a chair, and climbed onto it. He could barely reach the knot in the cord overhead and fumbled for an interminable moment before he got it untied. The room filled with yellow-suited figures who grabbed the body under and above John's arms and took its weight. "Get clear, sir. We've got him."

John backed away as the suits continued to work to bring him down. The man's head hung limp—he was gone. *Hmph. "Well looked after" my ass.*

John slowly backed to the door. The suits paid him no attention, and he slipped out and across the hall to Daniel's room.

---

"Daniel," John said, as loudly as he dared.

Daniel's eyes fluttered open as he woke from what seemed to be a peaceful sleep. He rubbed at his eyes. One of his hands sported an IV needle, tubes, tape, and other devices. Voices crackled in and out on John's helmet audio from the suits across the hall.

"About time you got here," Daniel said as he blinked away the remnants of sleep.

"Morning, son, how ya feeling?"

Daniel bolted upright. "What?" he grabbed John's nearest arm and stared through his face shield. "John! How?"

"Never mind that," John said. "How are you doing?"

"Okay, I guess," Daniel replied. "It's hard to remember, I've been kind of out of it. How long have I been here?"

"Three days. They taking care of you?"

"I... think so? I vaguely remember someone feeding me some kind of soup or broth or something. I feel pretty good, but I'm super tired, my back is killing me, and my head is pounding."

"Can you walk?"

"Yeah, I think so." Daniel swung his legs over the side of the bed. "Is Mel okay?"

John rummaged through the contents of a rolling cart and

found a set of standard gray clothes that appeared to be Daniel's size. "Last I knew. They arrested me a couple days ago." Static-clipped voices still bounced around inside John's suit.

Daniel stood and wobbled on his legs, a look of surprise on his face. Momentarily, he steadied himself on the bed.

"Here, put these on." John tossed him the clothes, then went around the room and tested the walls, which hung like curtains from the room's support frame. In the center of the back wall, where multiple sheets overlapped, it seemed possible to push through them into the next room.

Daniel slipped on the shoes and had the shirt over his head when the door parted and a yellow-suited figure stepped through.

"Going somewhere?"

John stepped up to the newcomer without hesitation. "Yes. I'm getting my son-in-law out of here." The two men stood, their face shields inches apart.

"John? I thought I recognized your voice over the audio."

"Nolan? Shit, son, am I glad to see you." John clapped him on the shoulder. "Help me get Daniel out of here."

"Not a great idea. The situation out there is almost cleared up and both ways out are going to be crawling with soldiers and staff."

"We'll take our chances." John grabbed Daniel by the elbow and led him toward the back wall.

"John," Nolan said, "if I heard you…"

The door parted and four yellow-suited figures poured through. The one in the lead gestured to Daniel, and one of the others headed toward him. "Get the patient back in his bed," the leader said.

*Harris.*

The lieutenant motioned toward John, and the other two

suits approached and held him by the elbows and wrists. "Did you learn what you needed to, Sergeant?"

"Oh yeah," John replied, "I've seen more than enough."

"I'm disappointed. You tried to take advantage of me."

"Of course I did," John said. "My daughter is out there alone. I should be with her. Her husband should be with her."

"Take him back to holding."

"John!" Daniel yelled.

"Get better, Daniel," John said. "We'll get you out of here." He caught Nolan's eyes, then let the soldiers lead him away.

---

# DAY SIX

## Paris

---

*9am, 29 August 2048*

*The sky is an infinite, featureless gray above the Jardin des Tuileries in Paris. A thick fog of fine ash, spewed into the air on the other side of the world, settles in drifts over the Place de la Concorde. In the distance, through the dark and the ash, the Eiffel Tower's beacon silently sweeps the enshrouded city.*

# ORGANIZED RESISTANCE

THE LOUNGE BUZZED AS MEL WORKED HER WAY TO A SEAT NEAR a large cluster of people. She recognized most of them, but knew only a few, like Jack and Celia, by name. Janie, the pregnant girl from Mel's floor, was here. Mel had asked around about her after the hallway fight outside her room and Mel's meeting with the counselor. Despite everything, Janie wasn't holed up in her room. *Like I want to be. Seems she's handling all this better than me.*

Unfortunately, little had changed in the four days since she and Tom had planted the first seeds of protest. A few had taken up the call, or at least pledged their support, but there were nowhere near enough to make a difference.

Meanwhile, building captains, counselors, or the rare officer who deigned to appear among them either ignored the rampant abuse, or pretended to listen and promised help that never came.

Most of those in the lounge seemed to have come just to bitch and moan about petty grievances. After the upheaval that shoved them all into this dank hole, after everything and everyone that it had taken from them, people still wanted to complain about the size of their rooms or the quality of the food, or to spread gossip about their neighbors. *When will these small-minded, self-centered little shits wake up?*

Mel tried to ignore the worst of it as she carefully negotiated herself onto a seat. The baby—and four nights in a strange bed—hadn't helped with her recovery from their grueling mountain crossing. She worried about bigger things, but if everyone else wanted to avoid the real issues—to stick their heads in the sand rather than face reality—that was their business. Maybe they'd already worked through the heavy stuff, and all they had left were daily annoyances and gossip. What place was it of hers to tell them how to deal with the end of the world? She stopped short of pitying them, or herself, though it gnawed at her. *Pity won't help us, and it won't get Danny back.*

The guy seated across from Mel was in the middle of a rant about the curfew, "there's no sun down here and it's not like we have anything to do, so why are they trying to force us all onto the same schedule?"

The young lady next to Mel spoke up. "My girlfriend was out after curfew last night," she said. "A neighbor saw them grab her off the street."

"They stuck me in a room with a guy they brought here without his meds," Jack said. "He started cutting himself and running naked up and down the hall. I called for the MPs, and they beat him up and hauled him off." He tried to hide it, but his expression was disturbingly smug.

A few seats away, Barbara said, "They took my son the day we got here. I mentioned he had Mono and my neighbor told the building captain. An hour later the MPs showed up, and still no one will tell me where he is or how he's doing."

"They put me in a room with two strangers," Janie said. "It was okay at first, but then they got in a fight and the MPs arrested them." Janie shared a look with Mel.

"They took my husband during processing," Mel said.

"He'd come down with the flu or something the night before, and by the time we got here, he was in such rough shape they just took him away."

Jack mumbled something Mel didn't quite catch.

"Jack!" Janie admonished him, and he looked away.

An older man said, "It been getting so you can hardly cross the avenue without being stopped, and if you say anything the MPs don't like, they'll arrest you too."

"And none of the building captains or counselors are worth a shit," Barbara said. "They keep saying they're 'going to look into it', but then either nothing happens or they report you for causing trouble."

A short, mousey kid said, "My neighbor said her friend from building five heard it's getting worse in Quarantine too. Apparently they're understaffed and running out of medications and just letting people die."

"I'm sure they're doing what they can," Celia said. "Like they said, there are too many of us and not enough to go around. They should separate out the troublemakers and the sick people—why risk the rest of us or waste resources on people who probably won't make it anyway?"

There were gasps and general expressions of outrage.

"What? If it's as bad out there as the reports suggest, we've got to make hard choices," she said. "And quarantine's not even a hard choice—" she looked directly at Mel, "if someone brought something nasty in here with them and it starts making the rounds, we're fucked. We might as well just lay down now." She slumped back in her chair and crossed her arms. "I just wish they'd give us something to do, so we can get the fuck over ourselves and move on."

"Maybe," Janie said, "if they'd give us straight answers, if they'd let us see what's really going on, it might not be as bad as we think."

"I don't see how roving squads of MPs beating up people

for no good reason could be 'not as bad as we think,'" Mel said.

"They have to maintain order," Celia said, "or all we'll have is chaos."

"Bullshit, Celia," Mel replied. "That's not order, it's fascism."

"Extreme situations call for extreme actions."

"Oh, for fuc…" Mel started.

"There's no excuse for treating people as less than human," Janie said.

"And yet," the older man jumped in, "we've seen time and time again how quickly and easily supposedly noble, enlightened people can treat others that way."

"And what happens when an apathetic community allows it to continue," Mel replied.

"So, what do we do?" Janie asked. "A couple dozen of us won't be all that threatening to a bunch of armed soldiers."

"We," Mel waved her finger in a circle to indicate the room, "are no match for the colonel's men. What we need is leverage. For the last few days a friend and I have been trying to organize a protest."

Celia threw up her hands. "This is a waste of time!"

"Maybe," Mel said, "but by joining together, we at least stand a chance of getting their attention, and, hopefully, if we keep our heads, without inviting more violence. I really think this is our best shot."

Janie and several others agreed aloud or nodded their heads.

"I'm sorry, Mel," Celia said, "but you're an idiot if you think they're going to allow this to happen. Already they're protecting us from ourselves, and you're just going to force their hand. They'll lock us all up for our own good and throw away the keys, and then where will we be? Your husband will still be in quarantine, and you'll be confined to your room. Is that what you want?"

Some of the others appeared to consider and even agree with Celia.

"I don't know if it's going to work, but I'm sure as hell not going to sit here quietly while they hold the people I care about and drag off more and more of us every day." Mel tore her attention from Celia and looked into the faces of those around her. "If there's a chance we can get them to reconsider, to change their approach, to work **with** us, rather than against us, then we **have** to take it! But to get their attention, it has to be **big,** and it has to be **loud**. Tom and I have been talking to people, but we've not made as much progress as I'd like. We need more voices, more people spreading the word."

"I'm done here," Celia said, and she and a few others got up and walked away. There were still at least a dozen left in the group, and they all seemed engaged, or at least interested enough to stay and hear what Mel had to say.

"We need to go to the other buildings and find supporters to help us get the word out. Who would be willing to do that?"

Six people, including Janie, raised their hands.

"Thank you," Mel said. "Talk amongst yourselves, divide up the buildings however you like, and go tonight or tomorrow morning. Try to recruit one or two residents who can work within their building. The rest of you should head to the mess hall or any other place where people gather and talk with whoever you feel comfortable. Try to convince as many as possible to meet us in two days at first meal time near the gates to the military compound." Mel breathed. "Thank you, all of you. Hopefully, together we can make a difference."

The conversations wound down and most of the people dispersed, except for Janie, who approached Mel.

"Hey, I… uh… I've seen you around."

"Mel Barber." Mel held out her hand. "And you're Janie, right?"

"Yeah, I… live down the hall from you."

"How far along are you?"

A young man lingered nearby, like he wanted to join the conversation, but was afraid to interrupt. She decided to ignore him for the moment and focus on Janie.

"Thirty-seven weeks, yesterday," Janie said. Her face seemed like it couldn't decide whether to smile.

"Wow…" Mel said, "wow."

"Yeah, she could come any time now, I guess. How about you?"

"Almost 21, nowhere near as close as you," Mel said. "How did you make the trip up the mountain?"

"I was at the hospital for a checkup." Janie lowered herself into the seat next to Mel. "My OB got wind of what was happening and she and a nurse wheeled me out to a group of soldiers who were gathering whoever they could find. I still haven't decided whether I should thank them, or… not."

Mel tried not to smirk. "Yeah, I get that. Feeling some of that myself, at this point." She patted her own smaller bulge of a belly. "Your roommates got arrested… you need someone to stay with til the baby comes?"

"No, I think I'm okay for now."

"Well, if you change your mind, let me know," Mel said, and glanced at their observer, who hovered a few feet away. "In the meantime, I think we have an eavesdropper." She jabbed a thumb in the man's direction, and his face flushed red.

He held up his hands and stammered, "Wha, no! I'm not… I was just…"

"Relax, I'm kidding!" Mel said. "Now, are you just going to stand there, or are you going to introduce yourself?"

"I'm Luke."

"Haven't seen you around here before, Luke. You in this building?" Mel asked.

"No, building four," Luke said, "but I spent the first few days with a group in another building. I wanted to get out and see what else is going on… see if I can help out in some way."

"What is it you had in mind?"

"Well, I don't really know anyone in my building, but I did make some… connections in the group I was with before, in building three." Luke blushed, his eyes fixed on the ground. "I might be able to talk some of them into joining us."

"That's great, but of course you can talk to whoever you like," Mel said. "You don't need my permission or anything."

"Oh, no, I'm not asking for permission," Luke said, "but I'd kind of like to have someone with me when I go. The situation with this group is… well, it was difficult to leave, and I don't want to get sucked back in."

"I'll go with you," Janie said.

Luke's face somehow grew even redder, and his eyes dropped to her belly. "Are you sure?"

*Oh, ho. Yes, it might be difficult to walk away from a three-day orgy.* Mel tried not to chuckle at how he danced around it. "I think I know the group he's talking about," Mel said, "and if I'm right, it could be a little… uncomfortable."

"Yes, I'm very pregnant," Janie said, "but I **can** walk, and I'm not having this baby **tomorrow**. You need backup. **I** can be your backup."

"Oh, uh… okay." He exchanged a pleading look with Mel.

"Fine," Mel said, "she'll be your backup, and I'll be **her** backup. Better?"

Luke smiled slightly and nodded.

"Alright then," Mel said, "shall we meet downstairs in about half an hour?"

Mel, Janie, and Luke met in the foyer of Building Two and headed toward Building Three.

"So, what's this group we're visiting, then?" Janie asked.

"Well, it's hard to say…" Luke said. "they don't really have a name for themselves. It's just people so scared of the end of the world that they…."

"Want to go out with a 'bang'?" Mel said and chuckled.

Luke blushed and looked away.

"Sorry," she said, "that was crude." She asked Janie, "Surely you've heard about the… orgy in Building Three, right?"

"Oh!" Janie said, her face also flushed, though it could have just been from the exertion of the walk.

It was only 200 or so meters between buildings, but Mel found it difficult to keep up a normal pace, and Janie was farther enough along in her pregnancy that she'd developed a distinctive waddle.

"I've seen some of them when they come up for air to retrieve supplies," Mel said, "but apparently our Luke here is something of an anomaly." Mel took Janie's arm protectively, leaned in, and feigned a whisper. "From what I've heard, once people go up there they don't tend to leave."

"I'm the only one who **has** left, as far as I know," Luke said.

"How many?" Janie asked.

"Hard to say," Luke said. "Hundreds, I would guess? Maybe as many as two-hundred?"

*Two-hundred?* Mel whistled. "Holy shit."

They entered the side door of Building Three directly into a stairwell, and Janie, winded, stopped with her hand on the rail. "What floor?"

"Third," Luke said. "You stay here. Mel and I can go the rest of the way."

"No," Janie said, "I'm going. Just give me a second."

The stairwell was identical to the one in Mel's building, but where her building's seemed cool and slightly moist like the rest of the cave, the air here felt warm and musty.

"Okay," Janie said, "Let's go."

They ascended the stairs—with Janie in the lead—and the air warmed and grew closer as they climbed. By the third floor landing, it was palpable. Out of breath and drenched in sweat, Janie reached for the knob and opened the door.

Pungent air washed over them, thick with sweet, smokey incense mingled with the musty, salty scent of sweat and sex. Janie gagged and turned away.

In the dim light of the hallway, naked people writhed in random piles on the floor or propped up in doors or against the walls. Some appeared to be wrapped up with others asleep, but most were engaged in some sensual or sexual act. Mel reached out to Janie, but she turned and ran back down the stairs as quickly as she could. Mel and Luke followed close behind. Janie gagged and her eyes streamed tears until she cleared the door into the cave and recovered her breath and composure.

Luke offered support, but Janie waved his hand away as she steadied herself against the building's wall. "You all right?" he asked.

"No… yes, I'm okay," Janie said.

"That's quite a… potent environment they've cultivated up there," Mel said.

"Feels like a sauna," Luke said. "I never quite got used to it."

"You stay with them long?" Mel asked.

"Longer than I should have," Luke said. "I didn't have the heart for it. I felt like there must be something more productive I could be doing."

"Well, I'm glad for that," Mel said. "I appreciate you volunteering to come back. If this group is as big as you say, getting their support would be huge, and it might help to have a familiar presence here when we talk to them."

A deep, warm voice in muted conversation filtered through the stairwell door, and Luke's gaze turned downward. The lightly tanned, well-toned man who emerged from the building seemed out-of-place in the drab gray environment, and Mel had to admit that, in this case, the voice was a pleasant preview of its owner.

The man's companions were a pale, doughy twenty-some-thing man and a slightly older, full-figured woman with rich brown skin. Their bodies glistened with sweat and radiated the scents that had driven Janie outside. They had thoughtfully, if minimally, covered themselves with common issue under-clothes. Outside on the street on a summer day, these three would have just been faces in a crowd, but in the cool gray of the cave Mel found herself drawn to them, almost mesmerized by their easy sensuality.

Mel took a small step backward to break the spell, and the group's leader politely pretended not to notice. He stood lightly, as if he might float away, his posture erect but free. His face suggested gentleness and warmth. Mel debated whether she was in the presence of some wise shaman, or merely one who'd spent too long playing among the waves.

"It is pleasurable to meet you," he said with a slight bow. "I'm Blaine, and these are my companions, Nora and Timo-thy." To Janie, he said, "I'm sorry if you found our community uncomfortable. Nora noticed your... difficulty, and we wanted to offer comfort."

Janie's face again flushed red, and her eyes darted away.

"I'm Mel, and this is Janie and Luke. And we're fine, thank you. There is quite a contrast between the cave and your... community. We were just a bit overwhelmed."

"I understand," Blaine laughed, and glanced at Luke. "Sadly, it is not for everyone. I and my companions have not withdrawn from the community's embrace since its inception, so we are accustomed. This cave, however, is as cold and barren as when we arrived. Well, except for the two of you, of course!" He beamed and opened his arms to Mel and Janie. "A vision of radiant fecundity!" He laughed joyfully and turned his gaze again toward Luke. "And Luke… it is a delight to see you again. Have your opinions of our community changed since you departed?"

Luke's shoulders stiffened under Blaine's expectant attention. "They haven't," he replied. "I still believe we can better spend our energies serving the world that's left, rather than squandering them in the community's embrace."

Blaine reached out to grasp Luke's shoulders and smiled an affectionate smile. "Good. Always follow what inflames your passions and commands your heart. That is the key to a happy, fruitful life."

Luke nodded, and Blaine embraced him.

"So," he said as he released Luke and returned his attention to Mel. "You did not come simply to glimpse our community and leave, nor did our wayward member return to reaffirm his decision to withdraw. To what do we owe the joy of your visit?"

"If you've not left your area since our arrival, you may not be aware of the military's increasing aggression or of the deeply concerning rumors surrounding the quarantine."

"We have heard of these things, but prefer a more intimate focus," Blaine said. "We derive happiness from union and seek only to shine our light amid this darkness through shared love and compassion."

"We are here," Mel said, "to propose a union of our own, to join with one voice against the aggressive and unreasonable quarantine and incarcerations. Your community is the largest among the survivors. Your support would bring enormous benefit to all of us."

"I understand," Blaine replied, "but we are content in each other and have no desire to engage in external conflicts. Our community provides all we need. The soldiers leave us alone, and if we do not challenge them, they will have no reason to challenge us."

"Of course, you and your community may make your own decisions, but the time will come when the freedom and autonomy you're currently enjoying **will** be challenged." Mel said, "The military take more to quarantine every day, and it's no longer just the sick, but anyone potentially exposed to them. It's only a matter of time before someone in your community becomes ill enough to require treatment and the military will break down your doors and haul you all off to quarantine and isolation until **they** decide how many of you we can afford to lose."

Blaine's gaze wavered, and some of the warmth drained from his face.

"You know she's right," Luke said. "They will come for you eventually—if for no other reason than the community doesn't fit their idea of normal."

Blaine was quiet for a moment, then raised his eyes to meet Mel's. "Perhaps. You may be right. But I choose to believe they will not come. We are no threat to them and enjoy our own form of quarantine from those who would seek to disrupt us. Thank you for your presence and for your concern, but please do not proposition us again. We are content to remain inside, together." Blaine bowed again. "Luke, it has been gratifying to see you again. You are always welcome within our embrace, should desire lead you back."

Blaine and his companions turned and re-entered the building. Some of his glow had faded—perhaps the constant cool of the cave had done it, but perhaps, Mel thought, it was her fault.

*WELL, here we go.*

Mel's heart raced as she stepped out onto the avenue from Building Two. For two days, she and a few others had recruited as many as they could convince to join the cause, and now it was time to make their stand. The handful of people on the avenue and headed toward the gates did not reassure her. *Small turnout then, I guess. Well, at least we tried.*

She flashed a weak smile at Janie and the few others who'd met up in the building's foyer.

"It'll be fine," Janie said, "you'll see." She patted Mel's arm.

More joined them as they walked toward the dining hall, but by the time they reached it, their group still numbered fewer than twenty. *Nowhere near enough to intimidate a platoon of combat-ready soldiers.*

The cave, as large as it was, tended to swallow sounds unless you were in just the right place, but a distinctive, water-fall-like sound grew as they neared the dining hall's far corner.

Mel scrunched her brow and tilted her head, focused on the sound. She'd entered enough packed auditoriums to recognize the warm burble of hundreds of conversations. Janie looked at her and grinned.

The meeting spot was around the corner and less than a hundred meters beyond the dining hall. The noise grew louder and clearer with each step. They rounded the corner and walked right into a small group who squatted, sat, or milled about, and chattered with each other. Beyond them, an enormous crowd had gathered.

Mel's breath quickened. *They came!* Her heart pounded. *Hundreds! Thousands? Holy shit!*

Tom and the representatives from the other eight building

stood at the edge of the crowd. They saw Mel and began to clap.

"No, please," Mel said and held out her hands to discourage them, "thank you." She shook hands with most and thanked them all.

Many in the nearby crowd observed her approach and greeting, and when Tom gestured to them, they slowly parted. Mel felt lightheaded and warm. Silence spread as the crowd continued to part and she, Tom, Janie, and the others walked toward the gates.

Near the front of the crowd, a sandy-haired man separated himself from a large group who stood apart from the rest. *Blaine!* He'd dressed somewhat more modestly in the bottoms from one of the shelter's standard gray outfits, and the rest of his group had covered themselves similarly, or more minimally, in bras and boxers.

"Your words touched us and we have come." Blaine took Mel's hands in his. "We realized that though we may fulfill our present desires, amid such suffering and through our isolation, the community's embrace may grow cold and our pleasure hollow. But by sharing our warmth with others, we may bring healing and enjoy continual renewal."

"I'm glad you're here," Mel said. "I hope that, with your help, what we do today will bring warmth, community, and healing for everyone."

Blaine bowed, and Mel and her companions continued to the gates where volunteers had assembled a makeshift platform in a pool of light from the cave's ceiling.

The small group of ascetics sat to one side of the platform, with their heads shaved, in minimal dress, and apparently deep in meditation. On the other side, dozens of soldiers stood in formation, at ease, with their weapons held down by their sides. Though still rusty with rank insignia, she recognized the sergeant's stripes from John's old dress greens and photos of her dad.

*Word's spread further than I thought, but all the better. Protest wouldn't be worth much if they didn't know about it.*

Mel turned to survey the crowd. A thousand people or more, all but a few dressed in gray, watched her expectantly, nervously eyed the line of soldiers, or carried on with their agitated, private conversations. A sense of anxiety and tension hung over the crowd.

Some of the protestors had found, or pulled from the compositors, material for signs on which they'd scrawled a broad range of slogans. Most targeted the quarantine, but a few promoted some pet grievance or another. For every three signs about the quarantine, another proclaimed "Meat is Murder," "Curfew = Control," "Stop the Lies, Open the Doors," "Kill The Fascists," "The End is Now," or other more or less sensible slogans.

At the back of the crowd, a commotion swelled as they parted once again, and faded as a squad of MPs carried a stretcher past the assembly, its occupant covered with a gray sheet. The crowd maintained a reverent, but brief silence until someone shouted, "Butchers!" and others echoed: "Butchers! Fascists! Close the Quarantine! Stop the Killing!" The crowd roared and pulsed as the MPs carried the stretcher past the platform and through the gates toward the medical facility.

Mel mounted the platform and held her hands up to quiet the crowd, which had grown since she'd arrived, and continued to grow as more people rounded the dining hall.

"Please," she shouted, "Everyone! Everyone, please!" It took over a minute for the crowd to quiet enough for her voice to carry beyond the nearest few people. "I know you're angry and hurting, we all are, and it is really… it's incredible to see so many of you here. Thank you all for being here to join our voices and stand together."

The crowd shook their signs and shouted their support.

"We all are suffering, every one of us," Mel said, "and now, in this most difficult time, the few loved ones we have left have been systematically taken from us! They won't let us see them or care for them, or even speak to them, and we have no way to reassure them that we're still here. We're told nothing about their condition or their treatment. We're told nothing about when they'll be released or when the quarantine will end. We're told nothing except that this is 'for our own good' and 'to protect the future.'"

From the crowd, more than a thousand voices rose in shouts against the quarantine and against the soldiers. She raised her hands again, and they quieted more quickly.

"This is not my future!" Mel shouted, and the crowd echoed. "I refuse to accept a future where a simple cold makes my husband a **problem** to be **contained**. I refuse to accept a future where friends and families are separated. I refuse to accept a future where a mother can't comfort her dying child in his last hours. I refuse to accept a future where any of us are treated with so little respect."

Mel took a breath, and the crowd roared.

"And..." she raised her hand again, "it is only getting worse! How many of your neighbors have they taken? How many of you are afraid to walk the avenue alone, or open your doors for fear that some soldier will beat you and take you away too?" The crowd shouted frenzied insults at the soldiers. "We lose too many every day. Every day, more of us give up even on the pretense of a life here, more of us decide that this isn't a life worth living. And how **can** we keep going when our so-called protectors have taken both our freedom and our dignity? Now is the time to take a stand and tell them that what they're doing is **not right.** Now is the time, before it's too **late** to fix it. If we don't stand up now, we don't stand a chance—

we'll either end up in quarantine or on a slab. So stand up! Let them hear you!"

A thousand voices washed over her. The soldiers stood their ground, but many fidgeted or stole glances back at their sergeant or their platoon leader who stood, tense and red-faced, behind their formation.

"So," she raised her hands and continued, in as loud a voice as she could muster, "we are here today to send a message—to show them we're not just going to play along anymore. We demand that they end the quarantine, they end their wrongful abductions, and they end their restrictions on our freedom. We will **not** sit by quietly. We will stand, together, against them. And we will defend ourselves!" The crowd cheered. "This is our declaration of freedom, but this is not a declaration of war. We are standing up to demand their respect, not to start a fight!"

The crowd's cheers broke and divided. Many continued to shout their support, while many more openly jeered, booed, or simply fell silent.

"We'll stay at the gate and continue the protest. We'll take our demands to the streets and remind them what we want at every opportunity." The crowd devolved into an angry, riotous mob, and Mel had to shout to be heard. "We'll stand together to defy them, and we'll stand together to encourage each other and to keep everyone safe! Stand together! Make them understand!"

The sergeant brought her soldiers to attention as the crowd slipped away from Mel like loose soil. They whipped them-selves into a frenzy, and Mel stepped backwards, instinctively away. *This isn't what I wanted.* Beside the platform, Tom barely contained his rage at the roiling crowd, while Janie's apparent calm was a transparent mask over her fear.

With the poor timing typical of a young officer, one of the company's butterbars stepped through the gate and approached the platform. Tom helped Mel down, and the crowd's outrage shifted to the Lieutenant. His gestures to quiet the crowd had almost no effect, but his next gesture brought an immediate response from the platoon leader, who commanded his troops with one word — "Ready!"

As a unit the soldiers raised their weapons, stocks to shoulders, muzzles pointed at the crowd.

*No! Don't do this!* Mel thought.

Those nearest the soldiers immediately fell silent or shouted and tried to scramble away. Panic momentarily focused and quieted the crowd, and the Lieutenant took the opportunity to be heard.

"I am authorized to make a statement," he shouted. "Hear me out! This is a military facility, and it is our mission to ensure the survival of our nation and its people. This is a vital mission of national importance, and we **will** fulfill it by maintaining order and containing any threats through whatever means we must." Shouts from the crowd grew. "The quarantine ensures the medical integrity of this facility, and we **will not** shut it down. Now, please disperse and return to your buildings. If you refuse to comply, you will be detained."

The crowd exploded with raised fists and voices, the soldiers and their rifles all but forgotten. The crowd beat like a heart, and the lieutenant stuttered. "Make n-no mistake!" he shouted, "Violence will n-not be tolerated! Further disorder will n-not..."

A fist-sized rock flew past the lieutenant's head from above, grazed his shoulder, and clattered off the makeshift platform.

Mel held her breath as pain registered on his face and he lost his shit and gestured to the soldiers who surged from their positions to stand between him and the crowd, their riot shields and weapons ready.

"No! Stop!" Mel shouted as she ran past the platform to stand in front of the line with her arms outstretched.

Almost as one, the ascetics rose from where they sat and filed over to form a line behind her. She turned her head to acknowledge and silently thank them as Blaine emerged from the crowd, followed by his community. He bowed slightly to Mel as they filled in the remaining space between the ascetics and the crowd. Behind them, most at the front of the crowd settled and grew quiet, though others weren't so quick to give up their anger.

Mel turned back and met each soldier's eyes. She stopped at their sergeant and held her gaze. "You can't do this. You can't."

The sergeant glanced over her shoulder at the lieutenant, who nursed his shoulder but held up a hand. "Hold!" the sergeant shouted down both sides of the line. "Hold!"

At the front edge of the crowd, people struggled to stay upright against waves from the back. Half of Blaine's people turned to face the crowd and tried to help those at the front keep their feet.

Another rock flew over their heads and struck the platform near the lieutenant. Tom grabbed the officer's sleeve and pulled him off the platform.

Mel ran to where they stood. "There has to be a better way to resolve this," Mel said. "It doesn't have to go this way!"

The lieutenant looked ready to pick up a weapon himself. "It's out of my hands!" he yelled, red-faced. "If they continue with this violence, we'll have no choice!"

"Of course you have a choice!" Mel shouted. "There's always a choice. It's your job to protect these people, not imprison or kill them. They're not soldiers, and you can't just control them like soldiers. They don't know you, they don't trust you," Mel said. "Show them they can. Please, take me to your commander. Let me talk to him. These people are hurting and afraid, at least show them you're willing to listen."

"I…" he stammered, then sighed heavily. "Fine. I'll take you. Not that it will make any difference."

Mel retook the platform and raised her hands to draw the crowd's attention. "Please! Listen!" *So many!* Mel wondered if the noise had finally drawn every survivor to the gate.

The crowd seethed, but turned their attention to her.

"They've agreed to hear us out!" Mel shouted. "I'm going to talk to their commander! Please, calm yourselves! Don't provoke them! Violence will only make things worse. I will make them understand. I will try to make them see reason."

"I've got all the reason in the world, right here!" The voice from somewhere in the crowd's midst preceded the large rock that flew over their heads and landed harmlessly, less than a foot from the lieutenant. A scuffle broke out in the crowd as they brought the thrower down.

"We'd better go," Mel said. "Their patience won't hold out for long."

"Stand down!" the lieutenant shouted to the sergeant, and gestured for her to report to him. He spoke to her briefly, and she saluted, jogged back, and shouted orders at the line.

The crowd pulsed as the soldiers lowered their weapons and followed Mel and the Lieutenant to the gate. Mel glanced back as they locked it and re-formed their line, and Blaine's followers fanned out to hold the space between them and the crowd.

Mel cradled her belly and ran, awkwardly, as fast as she could.

# DAY EIGHT

## Dubai

*8pm, 30 August 2048*

EIGHT DAYS ON, AND DUBAI CHOKES. THE SUNLESS GULF IS *unseasonably cold and thick with ash that has settled from the air or poured in through Shatt al-Arab and the Strait. The water undulates like wet concrete, as languid gray waves slosh up on empty beaches. A slush of ice and ash foams at the frigid edge. Nothing moves but the water in its cold, quiet futility.*

# LOOKING FORWARD WITH HOPE

THE SOUND OF THE CROWD FOLLOWED MEL ALL THE WAY TO the military building and echoed strangely around the cave. The building's plain gray face loomed ahead of them, and when they finally reached the single door, she stumbled in, winded, behind the Lieutenant.

The building appeared to be a simple concrete-block construction, but despite its age the interior walls were pure white, covered through the years in so many layers of paint that the underlying textures had been almost completely smoothed over, and the mirror-polished floors reflected the overhead lights until Mel felt snow-blind. She might have slipped and fallen on her ass if not for the ratty tread on her old hiking boots.

Every piece of furniture and equipment in the rooms they passed seemed to have fallen out of time, all gunmetal grays and flat greens and browns, as unblemished as the day they were made.

She remembered visits to the base psychologist in the years after her dad died—the cold, hard, metal chair against her legs while they asked their impossible questions. The memory ripped through her and hollowed her out all over again, and she shuffled after the lieutenant on that lost little girl's legs.

They climbed to the third floor, then turned left into another long stretch of hallway. A little farther along, a soldier emerged from a door and caught sight of the lieutenant. As they neared the room, the door slowly closed on walls of equipment and desks piled with metallic gray and drab-green boxes connected by tangles of wire. A brown plastic plaque engraved with the word "COMMUNICATIONS" was affixed next to the door.

The sergeant saluted, then glanced at Mel and stepped closer to the lieutenant to hand him a piece of paper. Mel tried to eavesdrop, but only made out the words "contact" and "D.C." before the two exchanged another salute and the sergeant turned to go back through the door.

The lieutenant continued down the hallway, and Mel jogged to catch up. They followed the hall to the right and walked another twenty meters to an oak door at the next corner. The lieutenant rapped three times on the door, then opened it and motioned for Mel to follow as he stepped inside.

"Lieutenant!" the colonel shouted before Mel was all the way in the room, "the corporal at the gate tells me we've got a full-scale riot on our hands! I thought I sent you out there to deal with it!"

"You did, sir, but the corporal exaggerates. There **were** over a thousand people at the gate with no interest in what I had to say, and the situation was escalating. This young woman stepped between the formation and the crowd, and several others followed her lead. She thought it best to speak directly with you before things truly got out of control."

"My officers should not depend on civilians to do their jobs for them, Lieutenant. You don't just walk away from a situation I've ordered you to handle."

"Colonel, Sir. You ordered me to handle it. You didn't specify how." The lieutenant's hands shook.

*More backbone than I'd have guessed*, Mel thought.

"In my judgement," the lieutenant continued, "the crowd is under control, but if we want them to stay that way, we should hear their demands."

The colonel hesitated, apparently as surprised as Mel was. "Well, you're here now," he paused again and looked at Mel. "Let me guess. You are Ms. Barber, the sergeant's daughter who's responsible for stirring up all this trouble in my facility?" He smirked.

"That's right." Undaunted by his rank or his condescension, Mel stepped toward the colonel. *Now's not the time to tread lightly.* "And since you know that, you surely know that you've held my husband in quarantine since we arrived, and you arrested my father for standing up against your thugs to protect me." Her face was stone, her voice a knife. "But I'm not **just** here for them. I'm here on behalf of all the survivors. We want the quarantine facility closed, the arrests to stop, and for our loved ones to be released. I'm here because your policies are more about control than protection—you detain anyone with the slightest medical concern, or anyone who simply disagrees with you, and it has to stop."

"My policies, young woman, are borne of necessity. The survivors arrived here sick or injured and in need of care. We provided that. You were frightened, distraught, and in need of comfort and stability. We provided that. You paid us back by complaining and arguing with us, by attacking one another, by killing yourselves!" The colonel was red-faced. "The quarantine is for your protection. To preserve the health and the lives of everyone in this facility. The people we arrested were troublemakers and thugs who threatened everyone's safety."

"My father wasn't a troublemaker—he is a soldier, like you, who stood up to defend me. My husband had a cold. A cold!

And you took him from me! We are all already captives, here. What about our freedom? Our rights?"

"I am concerned with the preservation of the human race!" Spittle flecked the colonel's lips. "We cannot tolerate sickness and violence! They will decimate the population and destroy any hope of humanity's future! I don't have the luxury of considering individual lives, or the personal freedoms granted by ideal times. This is it, **we** are it, and law and order are the only things standing between us and the abyss." He took a deep breath. "Lieutenant, fetch the sergeant from the stockade and bring him here."

The lieutenant saluted, turned on his heels, and left.

"I have, thus far, allowed your little group to come together," the colonel spoke low and quiet, "but my patience is gone. Your dissension and opposition won't be tolerated any further. It ends today," he stabbed toward the ground with his finger.

Mel's cheeks went cold under his gaze. What she saw in his eyes betrayed her hope.

*We are lost.*

Her head swam as images flooded past. All over again, Danny and John were taken, Janie cried at her little table, Tom hobbled on his crutch. She breathed, pulled herself up straight, and met the colonel's hard eyes with her own.

"Colonel, I have already lost my life, my freedom, and my hope, and you've taken the only two people I have left in this world. So, let me tell you, the only thing ending today is your little authoritarian fantasy!" She glared at him and spoke with careful intensity. "You can't win. You may keep some of us in line through force and fear for a while, but there are nearly three-thousand of us and only a hundred of you. In the end, you'll either have to kill us or make us prisoners. One way or another, we'll die. We've lost so many already, while you've been tightening the noose."

She took another step toward him. She smelled a hint of his aftershave.

"The people who showed up out there today aren't desperate and lost, they're strong and they're angry. If you push them to desperation, God only knows what will happen, and **you** will pay the Devil's price. The only way forward is to offer them hope. Give them something to live for, not more reasons to die." There was a quick knock, and the door opened behind her. The colonel's eyes flicked up to see who it was, but Mel kept her gaze on him. She felt certain that John was there, and his presence gave her strength. "But don't mistake me Colonel, I'm not here offering you a choice—the way I see it, you've already made your choice. I'm here to tell you that if you don't free our people, we will roll over you and take our freedom for ourselves. The question, Colonel, is how do you want to be remembered—as humanity's provider and protector in our darkest hour, or as the first footnote in our new history?"

She held his gaze until he looked away and gestured for the new arrivals to come further into the room. Mel glanced around. John's face was bloodied and bruised, and Mel sucked in a breath as heat rose through her face again. Her fist tensed, and she turned back toward the colonel.

John grasped her shoulder. "Mel," he said, "I'm alright."

She paused, relaxed her fist, and looked at him. Behind the bruises lay the calm compassion that had smoothed countless turbulent moments. Sadness she found there too, and pride, and, as always, strength. She turned to him, took his hand in hers, and quietly thanked him. She turned back and stepped toward the colonel.

"This man," Mel said, "is who **you** should be. He put his life on the line for an ideal. He stood with his fellow soldiers and he mourned lost friends. He took in a family that wasn't his, not just to fulfill a promise, but because it was the right thing to do. He stood back when it was appropriate and stood up when it was necessary. All my life he's shown me what he's made of, and he proved himself every day. So, Colonel, what are you made of? What do you stand for?"

Mel's gaze never wavered, and her challenge hung in the air.

The colonel sat back against the edge of his desk and pinched the bridge of his nose.

"This one is yours?" he asked John.

"I could hardly lay claim," John said, "but for whatever influence I may have had, she makes me prouder than any father has a right to be."

"Well, it's well-deserved." The colonel looked back to Mel. "I wish more of my officers had half your gumption. Certainly would make things more interesting around here." He stood and faced her. "But don't get me wrong, Ms. Barber, this is my hand basket and I have no intention of riding it to hell. We have contingencies within contingencies, and you apparently overestimate the value of the survivors to my mission." He walked around to stand behind his desk. "Were you aware, for example, that under the right conditions and restrictions one could build an isolated and sustainably diverse population from fewer than one-hundred people? We did not select the soldiers stationed here for their skills and psychological suitability alone —had we simply shut the doors and not taken in any survivors, they themselves were to be the seeds of a new civilization."

Mel's resolve slipped, and she looked back at John.

"So you see, Ms. Barber, we don't actually need you—at least not many of you. A hundred or so would be more than sufficient to safeguard against losses from accidents or other anomalies."

"Then why take us in at all?"

"Because that was part of the mission—a larger initial population and greater diversity makes some things easier. Of course, we expected to get scientists, thinkers, inventors, and builders, not Joe and Jane average. It seems the pinheads who came up with the contingencies we're operating under didn't consider the problems a generalized population would bring."

"Perhaps not, but they're not unsolvable problems," Mel said. "Relax your grip. Stop treating us like cattle. Stop arresting and beating us. Give us something to **do**. Give us a voice."

"She's right," John said. "The survivors won't feel settled until they have a sense of control."

"And release the people from quarantine," Mel continued. "Extra caution is understandable, but not indefinite imprisonment. If they're not contagious, let them go. It's not like you're going to stop people catching colds."

"I am not about to simply close the quarantine facility," the colonel said. "What I will do is review our protocols with my medical officers and determine an appropriate set of guidelines. In the meantime, we'll begin evaluating patients for release."

"It's a welcome gesture," Mel said, "but hardly suff…"

The colonel held up his hand. "If you'll let me finish, Ms. Barber. Ark protocols allow for—and under certain circumstances demand—that the people be allowed to self-govern. Our building captains, who we randomly selected during in-processing, have proved less helpful than I had hoped, and the officers on my staff have, thus far, been unable to gain the people's trust. So, if I am to, as you say, 'relax my grip,' I'll need someone I can trust—and someone the **people** can trust—to facilitate relations between my company and the civilian population." He turned his attention to John. "Sergeant, would you be willing to serve as a civilian liaison until we can help the survivors elect and establish a Civilian Council?"

Mel knew John well enough to see the calculation and emotion that played across his face as she fixed him with a stern, curious look. After the briefest of moments, the set of his jaw told her he had decided.

"I would," he said. "On the condition that you remain faithful to your word—that you will relax the quarantine and stop the aggressive detentions."

"You have my word," the colonel replied. "To be clear, until the council is in place, it is ultimately my responsibility to maintain peace and order among the survivors, and to maintain and manage the facilities **we've** provided."

"That's good enough f…"

Mel put her hand on John's arm. "Colonel, you have two days to evaluate and release the first patients and non-violent detainees," Mel said. "We will try to give you that much time to prove your words and get yourself back on the right side of this thing. After that," Mel trailed off, "well, we're survivors. If you think you can break us, you'll have a hard lesson to learn."

"Let's hope it doesn't come to that," the colonel said. "And it won't. My medical staff, in their infinite optimism, already provides a daily list. We'll identify the first potential group tonight and release those we deem safe tomorrow. For the rest of it, let's see how the next few days go."

The lieutenant cleared his throat and snapped to attention. "Sir."

"Yes, Lieutenant?"

"Sergeant Sanderson handed this to me earlier." He handed the colonel the piece of paper he'd gotten from the sergeant outside the communications room.

The colonel scowled as he took it, but his face relaxed as he scanned the report. "It seems," he looked up at Mel and John, "that we are, in fact, **not** the last of humanity's survivors."

Mel had never heard stranger words.

"We've just heard from Virginia," the colonel said, and smiled. "They have a full house."

"What?" Mel felt unable to comprehend the words, yet her eyes became heavy with tears.

"We've been working to establish communications with other known arks—with any group, honestly—government **or** civilian, but especially with the ark near D.C. Well," he grinned and smacked the paper, "we finally have! I think you'll understand that I have to excuse myself." The colonel headed for the door.

"Colonel," John said, "what about Mars?"

"Mars?" The colonel seemed genuinely surprised. "What about it?"

"The Mars colony," John said. "I have a daughter there. My grandsons are there."

"Hm." The colonel stood with his hand on the door. "I've not heard anything, but if they're out there, I'm sure we'll hear from them. Now, Lieutenant, escort these two to the civilian area and button things up—tell your people to stand down and pack it in. We have a lot of work to do."

The lieutenant snapped to attention and saluted as the colonel hustled out the door.

***

THE LIEUTENANT ESCORTED John and Mel out of the building, and when they reached the gate, they found chaos. The soldiers had donned their masks, drawn their weapons, and formed a semi-circle around three of their number. Two of them tended a third, who lay back on his elbows on the ground. Blaine's people and the ascetics still stood between the crowd and the soldiers. The crowd pressed, but the two groups worked together calmly and quietly to hold them back. It was a minor miracle the soldiers hadn't retaliated against the crowd and turned the mass into a meat grinder.

John and Mel ascended the platform, and after a moment

the crowd's focus shifted, and the soldiers lowered their weapons.

"The colonel has agreed to our demands!" Mel shouted over the burbling noise. *Mostly.* These people needed a victory, even a qualified one.

As she explained the colonel's plans, the crowd's mood shifted. They cheered the promised release of some of the quarantined or detained, and the ending of the curfew, but jeered and booed when she clarified that the quarantine would remain open and that the colonel's troops would continue to keep the peace. The crowd's reactions spread like waves, and Mel felt her own emotions being pulled out with them. The plans to elect a governing council, however, elicited only scattered support.

"Finally," she said, "I'm happy to bring news of a more profound nature. An hour ago, the Colonel's communications team established contact with another ark near DC!" She paused for a moment to let them process the news. "Others are out there! We are not alone!"

Shouts and cheers erupted from the crowd. Almost everyone laughed, hugged, or cried together. The soldiers doffed their masks and wandered through the crowd with broad smiles and clasped hands with everyone. The sound and the joy crashed over Mel like a summer storm. It was too much. Danny would be here soon, and her mind filled with thoughts of him.

## DAY NINE

### Northern California

*2pm, 31 August 2048*

Outside the cave, snow falls. Drifts cover the vehicles left behind and all but the very top of the enormous doors. The temperature has fallen well below zero. The air is pristine, cleaned by the falling snow. The leaves, branches, and trunks of trees not buried under or caked with snow are a uniform ashen gray. There is no life here, no color, only cold, and a distant sun straining to break through the blowing snow.

## LIFE AS WE KNOW IT

Mel wrung her hands to stop them trembling while a million thoughts tumbled and crashed white-hot in her mind until she felt both overwhelmed and utterly empty. She paced alongside the fence, past the gate and the guards.

John asked her, for the third time, to stop.

"Feet hurt," Mel replied, "makes them feel better." Her heart raced. *Couldn't stand still if I wanted to, anyway.*

"I think that's him, sweetie," John said.

Mid-step, Mel turned toward the fence. *Danny!* She hadn't seen him for a week, but she'd have known his casual gait if it had been a thousand years. Despite the monochromatic outfit some survivors referred to as "prison suits," he was every inch her Danny.

As he and his companion neared the gate, the soldiers opened it, and Danny rushed through and took her in his arms. He pulled her close for an intimate, passionate kiss.

Mel lost herself in his embrace and his lips. In the cave's cool air, his body felt so warm against hers, and his arms, wrapped around her in just the right way, made her feel safe and whole. She wanted to never let him go. Tears wet her cheeks, and their saltiness mingled with the subtle earthiness of his mouth. He relaxed his embrace just enough to look into her eyes. *Oh, God, I missed him just looking at me that way.*

"Hey sweetie," he said with a tender, butter-sweet smile. "Did you miss me?"

She melted all over again into his hazel eyes, and a single sob burst from her, almost a shout that she tried to hold back, and she laughed at herself as it died away. "Stupid goddamned hormones," she said.

The baby pushed against her ribs, and she winced. Danny looked at her, his eyebrow arched in confusion. She put his hand on her belly and buried her face in his neck to muffle her tearful laughter. "The baby missed you, too."

Mel didn't think herself prone to this sort of overt sentimentality, but she couldn't remember any moment when she'd been so overwhelmed at the sight of someone. She clung tighter to Danny as sobs poured out of her.

Mel cried for herself and her mother, and for John and June and their family, lost forever. She cried for Janie and her unborn baby, for Tom and Nolan and Luke, and for Blaine and his hedonists fucking their way to oblivion. She cried for those who didn't make it, who were outside dead or dying from whatever Hell had loosed on them all. She cried more for those who **had** made it, who now had to live without the ones they'd left behind—she cried for her mom and all those whose empty spaces would never be filled by the beautiful, radiant joy she felt at this moment. She cried for the empty spaces in herself that even this joy would never reach.

Danny said her name, and his voice, filled with concern, echoed in a world slanted sideways. She tried to focus, to surface from whatever she'd slipped under, but she felt comfortable and safe. She wasn't drowned, she was dead. Maybe that wasn't so bad.

"Don't leave me."

Her voice.

"I'm right here, sweetie."

His voice.

She felt his warmth, and she clung to it. Her body melted away, and the joy of him pulsated, expanded, and filled her up. It was enough that he was here. The rest would work itself out.

———

MEL AND DANNY waited impatiently in the reclamation room as the compositor slowly fused layer after layer of biopolymer foam into a solid object—the third leg of a crib they were building for Janie's baby.

Finally, together, they'd decided that they needed to do something—to make themselves useful. Their first target was Janie, or more specifically, her baby.

Mel had scoured the datanet to find plans for just the right crib, a task that had proved more difficult than she'd expected —*what's the right shade of gray for a baby's room? How does a crib not evoke a prison cell?* She thought it would be easier with Danny here, but darker thoughts continued to peck at her brain.

She wanted to surprise Janie, so she and Danny pulled crib pieces from the building's compositor and snuck them up to their room to assemble. Once they'd finished, they would roll it down the hall and present it to her.

Mel clung tight to the feeling, the anticipation of finishing something good, and of Janie's reaction. It was a light in the dark.

She and Danny sat in two of the room's three chairs, his arm wrapped around her, her head on his chest. "How much longer for this one?"

"About five minutes," he said, "for the compositing. Then another ten for coating and curing."

The compositor used the same material as everything else

the survivors had—the forks, the furniture, everything was made from and recycled into the same dense, featureless gray foam. Even the textiles, from their standard issue clothing to the stuffing in their sofas, were made from it through different processes and different machines.

Layers went down and Danny breathed. His breath was shallower than usual and his heart raced. Mel wasn't doing much better. In Danny's warmth, she'd recovered from the release of stress and emotion that had knocked her off her feet, but only somewhat. *Probably the same for all of us. We're all unsettled. On edge.*

A screen on the wall above the compositor occasionally emitted digital static—someone had neglected to turn off the news scanner.

"What's John up to today?" Danny asked.

"Helping wrap up the council election, I think. Vote counting or something."

Before the cave they had spent countless quiet hours together, none of them uncomfortable, but now there was a tension between them like stepping barefoot into a room where a glass has just shattered but you can't see any of the pieces.

The screen flashed to show an unrecognizable city street. The camera was half covered, the view obscured. Cars with open doors sat in snow or something that had piled against them in drifts. There was no movement apart from gusts of wind that disturbed the surface of whatever covered the ground. Danny got up and crossed the room to turn it off.

"You hear anything about who might win a seat?" he asked.

"Hm? Oh, nothing for sure, yet," Mel said. "I think Judy's a lock for our building, though. No way that idiot Gillet gets it."

Their first day back together had been great. They'd talked for hours, made love, and just existed in the same space until they felt like two parts of a whole again. When John came back that evening, the real world dragged them from their reverie and crushed them all over again.

Out in the old world, they'd loved to talk about their lives and about the future, but now there was the cave and then there was more cave—the cave was the present and the future, and as hard as they tried there seemed so little room for optimism.

So they latched onto Janie's baby and their shared secret task and tiptoed around everything else. Every moment she could, Mel buried her head in his chest, held him, and hoped it would be enough.

# FALLING APART

John sat toward the back of the new civilian council chambers. It was a small room on the first floor of Building Five, but the many empty seats suggested size wouldn't be an issue.

The turnout shouldn't have surprised him. Though the election process couldn't have been easier, only a third of the survivors had actually bothered to vote. It was disappointing and perplexing—but he didn't know if it stemmed more from apathy or hopelessness. John hoped the newly formed council would earn more support than the military had.

Among those in the room this morning, he recognized many of his fellow detainees—a vocal minority who had given the Colonel's troops a hard time. Many of the newly elected Council-members had, in fact, been part of that group as well. Mel had pushed him to run, but he had about as much use for politicians as he had for officers. *The real work happens on the ground.*

Still, the room was sparse, and among the few familiar faces were even fewer unfamiliar ones. He glowered at the empty seats. *It's the first damned session, people should be here!* He wanted to storm out, grab the first self-involved prick he found and drag them in by their ears to *pay attention and get involved, damnit!*

The door at the front of the room opened, and the ten newly minted council members, including his floor mate and building representative Judy, stepped through and arranged themselves behind a long table.

After the people—*well, a third of the people*—had elected their councilors, the council's first act had been to deliberate privately and select a chairperson. Their choice was one of the few John didn't already know.

Once the council had taken their seats, the chair rapped the gavel, and the room quieted.

"I call to order the inaugural session of the Citizen's Council of the Western Ark." the chairperson said. "We will begin with introductions and statements of background, for the record."

As the councilors rattled off their bios, John's thoughts wandered to Mel and Daniel. They were together again, but had struggled to regain their rhythm in this new world. For now, they busied themselves with their not-so-secret project and spent all their time together. It wouldn't be easy for them— nothing about this was—but he'd help them when he could, and he felt sure that as long as they stayed together, they'd figure it out. He and June had certainly gone through their own share of rough times and found their way through all of them together.

For his part, John had found some sense of purpose in his role as civilian liaison. He'd helped with the release and re-integration of patients from quarantine and detainees from the stockade. He'd assisted with the election process, and now that the council was formed, his own role was less certain.

*Card game nights with Judy and Marcus are fine and all, but if that's it...*

A few seats to his right, a lady he didn't recognize stood to polite applause. He clapped along absentmindedly.

His regular games of cribbage and gin rummy with some of the older couples in his building made his teeth hurt—not that he disliked them—they were nice enough folks, but it wasn't the same as **doing** something.

"… also on the Public Welfare committee," the chairman said. A couple of rows back, someone else stood to more applause. "The Civilian Oversight Committee will be headed by Councilor Reynolds." The chair invited Judy to speak with a sweep of his arm in her direction.

Judy stood and addressed the room. "The Civilian Oversight Committee is charged with oversight and regulation of the military, specifically as it pertains to the civilian population and our rights and responsibilities, as well as theirs." She continued, "The other councilors serving on this committee will be Thomas Sims and Rajesh Kalura."

John grunted involuntarily, *Rajesh. Good luck with that.* He'd infuriated John in the stockade with his inflexible insistence on seeing the worst of every situation. *But maybe it'll be good to have an obstinate pessimist watch dogging the military.*

The chairperson announced a few other committee chairs, who announced their members. By the time the last councilor had retaken their seat, nearly everyone in the room had been recognized. It seemed that only a few had come out of purely communal interest.

"That concludes the primary objectives of this session," the chairman said. "The floor is now open to questions."

A few raised their hands and were recognized, only to air petty grievances or inane questions.

*Things get this bad, and these jackholes still think of themselves first. At some point I'm going to have to stop being surprised by other people's selfishness.*

John raised his hand and tried to maintain a neutral

expression as the chairman passed over him several times to call on others until, finally, his was the only hand raised.

"John Hoffstead," the chairman said. "You have a question?"

"Of sorts," John replied as he stood. "Chairman... Parsons, was it? Councilors. Committees are all well and good, and there is certainly plenty to talk about, but it seems, with all this talking, there's been nothing said about taking actual action— of doing any actual work to address the community's needs." He paused, then continued. "I understand from the Colonel that there are plans for things we can **do** to improve our situation here, to ensure our self-sufficiency and better prepare for the future."

"You've seen the level of interest this community has in self-sufficiency," the chairman responded, as he indicated the room with a gesture.

"Well... again... politics are all well and good, but I think the Colonel and his people proved that governance isn't the solution to our problems. What the people need is hope. We *need* something to do," John said, "not to be sitting around bitching and moaning about the end of the world. We need work. We need a **future**."

"What do you have in mind?"

"I'd like to organize a work detail. A small one at first, cooperating with some of the Colonel's soldiers, to review and then handle practical implementation of the long-term occupancy plans," John said.

"You want to involve the military?" Judy asked.

"This is their facility," John replied. "In my role as liaison, I've found a few I know I can trust, and who we at least know can take direction. This would still be a civilian operation. I'm sure I can round up enough civilian volunteers to make it work."

The chairman looked at Judy, then exchanged glances with

the other councilors. All but Rajesh nodded assent, but despite the dark look he cast in John's direction, he didn't raise any actual objections.

"Very well," the chairman said. "You will report to Councilor Reynolds daily and take any proposals to the relevant committee for review before implementation. If there are any major concerns, I expect to be notified immediately. Now, if there are no further..."

The door at the back of the room opened loudly to admit a specialist who entered, winded, scanned the room, and double-timed it straight to John while the room burbled with quiet, curious chatter.

"Sergeant!" He spoke in an excited whisper as he approached.

"I'm retired, son. John's fine."

"John, uh, Mr. Hoffstead, sir, uh, Sergeant Hawthorn sent me to find you. Said you'd want to know. We, uh, we just got a signal. From Mars."

John grabbed the young man's shoulder. "Mars, you said?"

The soldier nodded. "The Sergeant thought you'd like to be there... if a message comes through."

"Damn right I want to be there!" John said. "But you'd better go tell them, first." He pointed toward the table at the front of the room.

The specialist walked to the front and quietly conferred with the councilors. Only a few showed any genuine interest. The young man returned, and John met him at the door.

"I'm all yours, son," he said, as they exited the room. "Lead the way!"

---

JOHN'S HEAD swam as he and the soldier ran the length of the cave, through the gate, into the military building, and to the communications room. When they entered, the sergeant looked up and motioned for John to come over.

"What's going on Sergeant?" John asked. "The specialist here didn't say much, just that you'd established contact with the colony?"

"That's about it so far," the sergeant replied. "We got a ping back on one of the standard frequencies about five minutes ago. Computer says we should be at about a seven and a half minute comms delay one-way, but their response time suggested an almost twenty minute round trip, assuming theirs was an auto-response to our last ping. It may be technical issues, or they're not actively monitoring their comms, or a response may already be on the way. My guess is we'll know something soon."

"Let's hope," John said. *C'mon, baby girl, tell me you're okay.*

Whatever destroyed the Moon and ravaged the Earth could have affected Mars as well. Life on Mars would be hard enough without a global cataclysm to contend with.

John pulled up an empty chair and had barely sat down when the equipment pinged and blinked to life, and an image of a bedraggled young man appeared on the screen.

*Earth contact, this is Tyler Leeds of the Mars colony.*

The young man looked like hell, like he hadn't slept in days. Or showered. Or eaten, for that matter.

*I apologize for the delay, but our communications array was damaged. We're still picking up the pieces here, rebuilding what we can.*

John and the sergeant shared a perplexed look as the colonel walked through the door. The sergeant silently motioned him over.

*The damage was extensive, and we... lost... seven colonists.*

A haunted look crossed the young man's face as he drifted into a momentary silence.

*Seven dead,* John thought, *Leana.*

On screen, Tyler gathered himself and continued.

*Some of our habitats, machines, and our primary greenhouse were destroyed, but we should have enough provisions to last until we can rebuild and reestablish food production.*

He paused again and seemed to search for his next words.

*We've seen feeds of what's happened on Earth, we've seen the destruction. Honestly, I'm not even sure if you're there or not, or if we just picked up an automated signal. If you are there, where are you? Who are you? Our current round-trip comms delay is about nineteen minutes, twenty seconds, and getting longer. Please respond, and let us know your status. Message ends.*

Without hesitation, the sergeant switched the equipment to record and transmit. "Mars Colony, this is Sergeant Hawthorn of the 675th Mission Support Group supporting the Northern California Emergency Sequestration Facility—an underground government survival shelter. We have around twenty-one hundred inhabitants here, settling in for long-term occupation. We've had intermittent contact with a similar facility near Washington DC." The sergeant looked to the colonel, who nodded toward John. "I also have a survivor here, John Hoffstead, with a message for one of the colonists..."

John stepped into the frame and cleared his throat. "Hey Leana, it's your dad. I imagine you're pretty surprised to hear from me, and I... I don't know if you're there to see this or not, but just in case you are… Mel and Danny are here with me, too. We're okay. We were out camping and just happened to be close enough to get the emergency beacon that brought us here. No one here seems to really know what's going on, but from what we've been told, it seems no one outside of a place like this could've survived. It looks like we're going to be here for a while, though, so we're trying to make the best of it. We've been here two weeks so far, and there've been some rough spots, but we're pulling together. I really hope you get this message, and you're alright, and that you and everyone up there are going to be okay. I suppose you're on your own now, so you're probably scrambling to prepare for that just as much as we are here. Hang in there, baby girl, and remember—whatever happens, I love you. Tell Luis and the boys I love them too."

John stepped out of frame, and the sergeant scooted back in.

"Mars Colony, if Sergant Hoffstead's daughter is there, please see that she gets the message, and that she gets a chance to respond if she's able. John here has been harassing us to get in touch with you all, so I'd really appreciate it if you could make that happen and get him off my back." He winked at John. "We'll await your reply."

The sergeant flipped the switches to end and send the transmission, and set receive mode.

The colonel pulled around a chair and sat. "Nice work, Sergeant. So, twenty minutes at least before we get a response?"

The sergeant nodded.

"I appreciate you letting me sit in on this, Colonel," John said. "If there's even a chance she's alive…"

"You two are close?"

"Yeah, well, I was upset when she and Luis decided to lead the Mars mission and take my grandsons with them, but my wife softened me up, as she usually did when the kids did things

I disagreed with. We were at the launch when they left. We've talked often since then, actually talked to her just before all this… but, well, it feels like it's been forever."

For twenty minutes they talked about family and shared embarrassing stories about people they'd trained or served with. It was the way in the military, to a certain extent, though the conversation seemed more raw than John remembered. Like everyone else here, these men had probably left their own families and friends behind as well. All of them now had to cope with tragic losses. If they were to move beyond this, if this was to work, they'd eventually have to bridge the divide between civilian and soldier.

Twenty-three minutes and a seeming infinity of seconds after their message, the equipment once again blinked to life and John recognized Paul Robinson's tired face, a little older and lined by stress.

*This is Paul Robinson, Chief Councilor of the Mars colony. We can't express how relieved we are to have received your message. We heard of the possibility of shelters such as yours, but when we hadn't heard anything after the first couple weeks, and the Earth satellites we hijacked didn't reveal anything, we feared the worst. As Tyler mentioned in his message, we've been tracking things on Earth, and tracking the Earth itself as it turns out. We're aware of what happened, though we're still a bit hazy on what caused it.*

*Tyler also told you about our own recent struggles. The object, whatever it was, has apparently pulled Mars into a tighter orbit. We've had a rough time of it. We lost some good people.*

Paul struggled to keep his composure.

*John, I…*

Something off camera distracted him and he leaned off screen. The signal cut off.

John's heart dropped like lead. The blank screen pulled at him like a black hole. Then, as suddenly as it had gone dark, it brightened, filled with another face. John almost didn't believe his eyes.

*Dad! Holy crap, Dad! I can't believe it!*

Leana. *Leana!* John's throat closed around her name, and he struggled to swallow the sob or shout of joy that threatened to break through.

Leana burst into tears.

*Dad… I…*

*She can't even look at the camera.* John ached to hold her and tell her he loved her.

*We were so close.*

She sat up straighter and looked at the camera.

*We're still recovering, getting the HABs resettled. The boys. The baby! Oh, the baby is doing great, Dad, thank God. Just a few more months, now.*

Tears ran down her cheeks again, but she held it together.

*Gabriel, he's so little still, I don't think he understands what's happened. And Michael… Maybe soon, maybe you could send them a message? Maybe you could talk to them?*

John looked at the colonel, who nodded.

*Oh, Dad, I can't believe you're alive! It gives me hope, knowing you're still out there. I love you.*

She glanced offscreen, annoyed.

*I need to give you back to Dr. Robinson. Seems we're about to lose the relay satellite we're using to talk to you.*

She stood up and her baby bulge filled the camera. Then she leaned back in.

*Oh,* and give my love to Mel and Danny, too! We'll talk again soon. Love you!

John had only seen her framed in relative close-up since the baby had started to show, and her progress caught him off guard. For the thousandth time, he lamented her decision to fly off to Mars. *But at least she's safe, probably safer there now than if she'd stayed.*

Dr. Robinson re-entered the view and sat.

*I do have some potentially disturbing information to share that you may not yet be aware of. As I mentioned, we've been tracking you, and it's clear that the Earth has also been pulled out of orbit. There's still some uncertainty in our calculations, so we've not yet been able to determine to anyone's satisfaction whether you've been pulled into an extreme but stable orbit, or if Earth will actually end up being ejected from the solar system altogether. Whatever the case, we're monitoring as best we can now that our comms array is back up, and we should still be able to communicate periodically for quite some time, though with an increasing delay. I don't know what expertise you have there, Sergeant, but we'll send our data along with regular status updates, and we hope you'll do the same. Until our next message, our thoughts are with you. Good luck. Mars Colony, out.*

For a moment, no one spoke.

"Sergeant," the Colonel said as he stood, "send that message to myself and the rest of the cadre, and to the Citizen's Council, please. And send it to the DC Ark if you can. Scratch that. Do whatever you need to do to broadcast that message to **anyone** left who might be listening. We don't have the luxury of old ways of thinking." He put his hand on the sergeant's shoulder. "And please send the relevant parts to Sergeant Hoffstead here, so he can view it again on his own. Congratulations, by the way—Grandpa," he said. "Thank you both. We've got a lot of thinking to do." He left the room.

"Or a lot of digging," John said. "If we've been pulled out of orbit, it won't be long before everything on Earth freezes. Our only hope is to go deep, get away from the cold and closer to the core."

The sergeant stared, glassy-eyed, at the screen.

"We're not dead yet, soldier." John squeezed his shoulder. "There's still hope."

## COMING TOGETHER

MEL SAT NEXT TO JOHN AT THEIR KITCHEN TABLE. ENGROSSED in a mountain of binders, John furiously tapped notes into a slate.

"You making any progress with that?" She took an orange from a bowl of tiny aquaponic fruit.

"Hm," John grunted. "I had forgotten how maddening Army procedural documentation could be."

Behind Mel, Danny leaned against the kitchenette counter. "Looking at that mess, I can believe it."

John had been obsessed for days, since "that do-nothing Council" meeting and the surprise call with Leana, which he'd immediately shared with her and Danny.

"They have scenarios, protocols, prioritized action lists, but nothing easily generalizable outside of their anticipated parameters." John flipped through several pages and threw up his hands. "So I'm trying to pin down a sequence that will let us move further underground without compromising our resources."

"The colonel's people can't help with that?" Mel peeled her perfect little orange.

"They keep going in circles trying to make one of the prescribed scenarios work, but none of them reach the right outcomes early enough or in the right order. The news from Mars has gotten around, and morale has taken a nosedive—the people are losing hope. I said I'd work on it and bring them something tomorrow."

"By yourself?"

"Judy's coming over in a bit, and the lieutenant who knows the most about what we've got to work with. We'll hash it out together, but I wanted to get a head start."

Mel felt Danny behind her. His presence was a comfort, but something still held her—a darkness that neither hope nor Danny could brighten.

"So, what are we looking at?" Mel asked. "You have any idea what work crews you're putting together first?"

"So far?" He glanced at his slate. "Well, we need to get the Hydro Plant up and running. Output from the solar farm is down significantly, either because it's damaged or obscured, or just because we're getting farther from the Sun."

"We'll only be able to run generators for so long unless we develop another fuel source. We've got to have the juice to do the work we need to do, and we need to move our water resources from above-ground where it will freeze and get it down here with us." John shuffled his binders and poked at one. "We need a Structural Engineering team to help the Colonel's group dig and build deeper, and we need to increase our food production—our existing aquaponics and protein culturing facilities are at capacity already, and our shelf-stable supplies will only last a few years, maybe five if we stretch them. I think our first work detail has to be construction."

Danny rinsed his cup and set it upside down in the dish drainer.

"You two, though," John began and chuckled, "I saw that crib, so probably not construction for you two. Maybe..." he rummaged through the layers of binders, pulled one out, and held it out to Danny.

Mel and Danny had delivered the crib for Janie's baby a few days ago, and they hadn't yet settled on another project. Without something productive to do, an uncomfortable tension had taken root between them.

"Hydroelectric Plant Operations?" Danny read.

"The soldiers can handle the engineering, but I think you can figure out enough to coordinate and manage the process."

Danny sat and flipped through the first few pages. "Looks complicated."

"Everything you need to know should be in there," John said. "If there's something you don't understand, the colonel's people can help. You'll want to meet with the team as soon as possible."

"I *am* tired of just sitting around." Danny's eyes flicked in Mel's direction, but dropped back to the binder just as quickly. "I need something to do. Some way to help."

*Ouch.* Mel sighed. "You have anything for an artist, or perhaps a highly qualified cashier?" She tried to keep the hurt from her voice.

"We'll need everyone we can get on the engineering and construction crews," John said. "You interested in some good old-fashioned manual labor? Tunneling, crushing rock, building buildings, that sort of thing?"

"Yeah," Mel patted her pregnant belly, "maybe not. You going to have a painting crew? This place could really use some color."

"I haven't seen anything in here about painting. I guess color wasn't a high enough priority." He flipped the bulk of the binder's pages over onto one finger while his right hand hunted near the back for the index.

"Fair point," Mel said. "But I am getting a little stir crazy here myself. You're busy, now Danny's going to go off and do whatever…" She got up and took a cup from the cabinet, then filled it from the faucet.

"There aren't exactly many jobs available," Danny said while Mel drank.

"Yeah, that's part of the problem," Mel said. "Am I supposed to sit here all day gossiping with old ladies and layabouts? Things were supposed to get better, but they're not! I need something to do too!"

"Sure… of course, sweetie," John said. "We'll find you something."

An image flashed through Mel's mind of her mother bent over a flower bed. *Mom's hands were never idle long.* She tended those beds for hours each day, and her modest little home always seemed nestled in the heart of paradise.

"You said we're going to need more food, right?" Mel asked.

"Yes…"

"And obviously there are seeds and supplies…" she added.

John seemed skeptical, but Danny's face had lit up. "A garden! Mel, that's perfect!"

"A garden?" John asked. "I don't know."

"It doesn't have to be huge," Mel said, "just something to bring a little more life into this place, a little more color."

"Well, I'm sure we can find some volunteers to help, maybe build planters and work up some soil. I just don't know about seeds. I'll have to talk to the aquaponics team."

"That's fine," Mel said. "Just do what you can." She paused for a moment and closed her eyes, then looked at him again. "I think I want this, John. I think this will help… people."

"Then you've got it," he replied.

MEL PLUNGED the trowel deep into the loose new soil and worked up a small area. She poked small indentations into the turned earth, dropped a few seeds in each, and covered them over. Mel didn't have a floppy hat or a floral-print dress like her mom used to wear, but she had dirt up to her elbows and caked under her fingernails. She caught the scent of the soil and smiled.

When she was little, Mel would play in the backyard in the evening while her mother tended a small raised bed. In late spring, early summer, the garden would be a lush, beautiful thing despite its size. Mel loved the smell of the flowers, lavender, and herbs, and she loved to pick cherry tomatoes when her mother wasn't watching and squeeze them between her teeth until they popped. The crunch of the skin and the sweet tang of the juice had defined her summers for many years.

"Hey sweetie, I'm done with this corn... the Bantam seeds." John said.

"Oh, great." Mel gestured to the beds on the other side of the gate. "Then I'd say get started with the White Cloud variety over there. Same drill." Mel smiled. John had taken time away from his many projects to help with hers. It almost felt like old times.

"You got it." John picked up his hoe and bucket of smaller tools and carried them over.

John had found volunteers to build raised beds in the area between the gate and the dining hall—the same place where, only two weeks before, the community had come together to stand against the colonel and his soldiers. The garden would be out of the way here, but not so far as to be forgotten.

Gardening had always been her mother's thing, so Mel didn't know much, but some of the volunteers knew a little and the ark's botanical database had all the specific information she needed.

The ark's seed vault was meant to enable species recovery

after a disaster or to be an emergency resource for the aquaponics team, so it had taken some effort to secure enough seeds and supplies to get started. Mel had convinced them that the garden would be not just practical and productive, but beautiful as well.

The aquaponics facility was like a tightly controlled factory installation, and its strictly managed nutrient and water cycles allowed highly efficient food production and helped to clean their air and water. Mel's garden would do some of that as well, though in a much less efficient, more organic fashion, and it would be visible and accessible to the people. It would be a symbol of hope and a literal example of how life could flourish in this dark place.

Footsteps echoed off the cave walls and Mel turned her head as four soldiers emerged from around the corner of the dining hall, a stretcher suspended between them, the body draped with a sheet.

Tears welled in her eyes. Despite their efforts to make things better, suicides had increased. Darkness and isolation took their toll, and fear did the rest. It gnawed at Mel every day. She stabbed the soil and opened it. She dug for hope because they were all buried in despair. Mel wiped away her tears and dropped a few seeds into the fresh hole.

Squash, watermelon, green beans, tomatoes, potatoes, cabbage, lettuce, and even corn were on her list, along with Calendula, Daylily, Nasturtium and a few flowering herbs. Flowers would serve little purpose below ground beyond their visual appeal, so though Mel had included mostly edible species, it had been especially difficult to negotiate their release. She would make this place beautiful. *Hopefully, a little beauty will make things more bearable.*

Somewhere in the cave, a scream.

Mel closed her eyes. *When will it end?*

The sound that followed the scream, though, seemed

unusual, like a car crash. A spike of pain struck deep inside Mel's left ear and made her gasp. She instinctively opened her mouth and pressed her fingers against the back of her ear. *What the hell?* Whatever it was, it stopped almost as quickly as it had come, though her ear still rang a little.

Then there were wheels on the dusty cave floor, and the crunch of footsteps. Finally, Mel looked up.

A soldier pushed someone in a wheelchair around the corner of the dining hall. The woman in the chair cried out in pain as they rolled toward the gate, and Mel dropped her tools and cleaned her hands as best she could on her clothes. She shouted to John, "It's Janie!"

John rushed to open the gate, and Mel ran to meet the wheelchair. "Janie, I'm here! I'll come with you."

Janie sucked in a pained breath and nodded.

As they passed through the gate, Mel called to John again. "Tell Danny what's going on. I'll try to make it home for dinner if I can!"

John closed the gate behind them as the soldier pushed Janie across the cave toward the medical facility. They burst through the double-doors of the main entrance and the soldier hit the override to open the inner doors. They swung out into an open area, and a startled nurse looked up, quickly assessed the situation, directed them to Surgical Bay 1, and picked up a handset.

By the time they reached the door, a small entourage of nurses sprinted to join them and follow them in. One of them helped Janie stand and asked the soldier to wheel the chair out of the room. The nurse helped Janie out of her clothes and into a gown, then dropped her clothes into a bin marked for the textile recycler.

"Breathe, Janie," the lead nurse said.

Janie was closer to term than Mel, so the staff had gotten to know Janie well during her weekly checkups since they'd arrived. Mel, in her obsession to free Danny, hadn't managed to make time for a single visit.

Janie breathed quickly, heavily, and she grunted as they helped her onto the edge of her bed.

"Lay back," the nurse said, and helped Janie the rest of the way onto the bed. "Now, I'm going to determine the baby's position." She pressed hard enough at various points on Janie's distended belly that Mal flinched. "Okay. Janie, your baby hasn't turned yet. We're going to try to encourage her to turn. Ron, get the doctor, please." One of the other nurses left the room, and then, aside from Janie's sounds of discomfort, it was quiet while the nurses that remained attached sensors to her belly, chest, and a fingertip.

Moments later, the doctor entered from the room's side door, scrubbed and gloved, with the nurse right behind her. The others in the room nodded and moved out of her way to their respective positions. It felt like orchestrated second nature, but still it occurred to Mel that this team had probably never delivered a baby here or together before.

"OK, Janie. Here we go," the doctor said.

Janie winced as the doctor pushed and poked at her belly.

"The baby's heart rate is dropping," a nurse said.

Janie whimpered, "What does that mean?"

At the same time, the doctor said, "Raise her right side, please."

The nurses rolled Janie slightly onto her left side and slid a long pillow under her back and hips.

"It's OK Janie," the doctor said quietly, "it's nothing to worry about. We're almost there." The doctor pushed on her belly again, and Janie grunted and huffed under the pressure.

*What are we doing here?* Mel wondered. *Who are we kidding?*

Finally, the doctor stopped and rested her hands on Janie's belly while the baby moved visibly inside. "There we go. Good job, baby girl."

*How fucking selfish do we have to be? Bringing another life into this place?* Mel's hands touched her own belly, noticeably bigger now than when they'd arrived at the cave.

"Heart rate is good."

*Do we really think we can outlast this sadistic universe that obviously has it out for us?*

"Excellent. Now, that wasn't so bad, was it?"

"Maybe for you," Janie said, her voice weak.

There was nothing behind or ahead but tragedy and struggle. A fight for every inch of space, every flicker of light, every bite of food. *What **right** do we have? How **dare** she! How dare **I**? Fucking selfish…*

But there was no arrogance or even hope in Janie's eyes. Right now, there was only pain and fear.

Mel stepped closer to the bed, took her friend's hand, and held it quietly. Janie didn't look up or acknowledge it except through the tears that streamed down her face.

A commotion outside the room broke the momentary quiet. Boots pounded the floor as a gurney rattled past. A nurse left the room, then returned a moment later. "There was some kind of accident at the… hygroplan? They're bringing in two DOA, and two others."

Past the nurse, through the surgical bay's double doors, a familiar gray-haired figure approached the nurses' station.

"Ping Doctor Tramontana and get him here," the doctor said.

Mel barely heard the exchange, as her entire being focused on the man outside the room on the other side of the door. He turned, and in partial profile his lips moved and gave focus to the familiar sound of his voice and helped her pick it out from the noise despite the great divide between them. *John?*

"His wife is here somewhere. Find her."

Mel instantly understood, and her heart froze in her chest. She couldn't breathe or swallow, and as the door closed behind the nurse, John turned toward her and met Mel's eyes. Pain. Recognition.

Mel dropped Janie's hand, ran to the door, and burst through it.

"Mel!" Janie. Worried.

John's eyes locked on hers for just a moment, then darted toward another set of double doors several feet away, where the nurse disappeared. John started toward her, but Mel turned, ran to the door, and burst through.

"Ma'am!" A different nurse shouted at her from a few feet inside the room. "You can't come in here!"

Behind the nurse who moved directly into Mel's path, a soldier and another nurse lifted a figure, slack-jawed and covered in blood, from a gurney onto the surgical table.

"Danny!"

The nurse pushed against Mel's shoulder, and the nurse Mel had followed in quickly joined in and now also tried to hold her back. The private watched closely, but remained out of the way near the wall.

"That's my husband, damn you!" Mel pushed through and rushed to his side. "Danny!"

"Oh, hey, babe." His voice cracked, and he raised his hand toward her, though his eyes stayed closed.

"Hey yourself," she said, and took his hand.

On the other side of the table, nurses cut through his clothes and placed biosensor patches on his chest.

"Damnit, Danny, what the hell happened?"

Machines came to life around him. "Jack?" Danny mumbled. "How's Jack…" he trailed off and his face went slack.

"Danny!" Mel squeezed his hand while the machines continued to beep reassuringly. "Oh, Danny."

The door at the side of the room opened to admit a doctor, another nurse, and a muffled, but clearly pained shout from

Janie in the other room. The doctor looked Danny over, pushed on his stomach, listened to his lungs and heart, looked in his ears, and shined a penlight in his alarmingly bloodshot eyes.

"There are no obvious external injuries." The doctor glanced up at the lead nurse, who shook their head. "He presents as though he's been near some kind of explosion." To the soldier, the doctor asked, "do we know what happened?"

"No sir. We got an alert from the hydro plant, and multiple calls reporting an explosion, but apart from this gentleman and the others we didn't find any evidence of one."

"Thank you, Corporal, you're dismissed." The doctor looked at Mel as the soldier quietly left. "Mrs.?"

"Barber."

"Mrs. Barber, your husband has symptoms of blast wave injury, and I'm betting he has a concussion. We'll get a head CT and perform other tests to be sure, but so far his injuries appear mostly superficial. His eardrums have ruptured, and he has burst capillaries in his eyes, but neither appears severe enough that I'm concerned about significant permanent vision or hearing loss. His breathing is regular and clear, so his lungs seem good, but we will get scans there as well, just to make sure. With this type of thing, it can sometimes take hours or days before the true extent of the damage becomes apparent. My biggest concern right now is internal abdominal injury," he paused, "so we'll get a quick ultrasound to look around and see if there's any reason for immediate action, and we'll take more detailed scans later to rule out anything else." The doctor nodded to a nurse, who left the room and returned moments later with a rolling equipment cart.

Danny moaned and muttered, and floated in and out of consciousness as the doctor applied the gel and manipulated the ultrasound. Every time he opened his eyes and looked confusedly around the room, Mel focused on his face and watched and hoped with every molecule in her body for him to smile at her. He washed ashore and back out again, and she held on.

A muffled scream made it through from the other room, and the doctor asked a nurse to see if he could help. He handed the ultrasound device off to another nurse, who cleaned and put it away while he wiped excess gel from Danny's stomach.

The nurse returned. "She's at ten centimeters, and making progress."

"Okay, thank you." The doctor removed his gloves. "I've done everything I can for the moment. Danny's ears should heal on their own, though he may have a little trouble hearing for a few days. But if he has any other issues, let us know. I'm going to assist Doctor Beck with her delivery, and a nurse should be here in a bit to take Danny for his scans." The doctor left the room, and the nurses followed shortly after.

Mel squeezed Danny's hand, and tears welled in her eyes. "Damnit, Danny."

The door opened, and someone entered. "Mel, is…" John started.

"No!" Mel surprised herself with the ferocity of her reaction. "Just… no. He is here because of you! You pushed him into this, and now he's here, and I had just gotten him back, damnit!" Her throat clenched around the words. "You don't get to talk to me right now. Please, just leave."

"I'm sorry." John said and left the room.

*We're all sorry, aren't we? Should have stayed on the mountain. It shouldn't be like this.* Mel closed her eyes tight and stomped her foot. *Damnit!*

A cry of pain from the other room brought Mel back. She wanted to be there for her friend, but Danny needed her too, so for the moment she held his hand and listened.

Janie cried out again—a sustained cry that ended abruptly

and was followed by the piercing wail of a baby's newly cleared lungs.

"Don't they know people are trying to sleep?"

*What?*

Danny squeezed her hand twice, and she looked down at their intertwined fingers, then at him.

*He's awake!* "What?" Mel asked.

"I'm trying to take a nap here." He slurred the words, but he grinned up at her.

She chuckled despite herself, though it sounded more like a strangled blubber, and she pulled his hand to her face as her tears fell all over again. She sniffed and laughed and finally opened her eyes. His smile was beautiful.

"So, what'd I miss?" he asked.

The baby cried out again, and Danny looked genuinely amazed. "Oh," he said.

He looked so pleased, and the baby sounded so desperate, and tears ran down Mel's cheeks.

"Hey now, let's not start that again," Danny said.

"It's just…" Mel started, "it all seems so… pointless."

He squeezed her hand.

"I mean, what can we offer that little girl in there? What kind of world are we bringing her into?" She glanced at him, but she couldn't meet his eyes.

He looked straight at her, but his eyes seemed lost. The baby cried, and he seemed to focus.

"We offer her the only things we have," Danny said, his attention now fully on her. "We offer her hope, and family, and community. We teach her," he reached over and put his other hand on her belly, "and those that follow her—that you don't give up even when things seem hopeless. Things change and no one can predict the future, but we can only make it better if we meet the moment and keep making the effort."

"It seems we might have to learn that ourselves first," Mel replied.

---

In Danny's room, Mel sat quietly by his bed and read from the slate the nurses had brought her to help pass the time. In the next room, Janie cooed at the baby.

They'd moved into adjacent rooms in the former quarantine area, per Mel's request and Janie's insistence, and over the past couple of days everyone had adjusted to their new routines, though they had yet to convince the baby of that.

Nurses and doctors came and went, they took measurements, drew blood, and administered drugs. When everyone felt up to it, they'd pull the curtains aside and share one big open space.

Occasionally, Danny retreated into his head—a worrisome new habit which Mel had yet to get him to open up about, though she suspected the cause. Jack hadn't made it through the first night after the accident, and Danny had taken it pretty hard. The Specialists assigned to the Hydro Plant detail hadn't even made it out of the cavern. It wasn't hard to guess why he seemed so haunted.

Someone tapped on the plastic entry to Danny's room, and Doctor Tramontana entered almost immediately after. "Hey, you two... how're you feeling?"

"Like I'm on a suborbital to Sydney," Danny said.

"Still?" The doctor put down his slate, pulled a scope out of its holder, and held it up to look in Danny's ear. "Mmhm," he said, and switched to the other ear. "Hm. Yep. You're healing up nicely, but there's still some inflammation. I'd expect you to start feeling a bit more normal in a few days." He sat somewhat casually on a nearby stool. "But, I didn't come by to talk about your ears." He looked toward Janie's area and jerked his head toward the open curtain. "You want me to close that?"

"Nah," Mel said, "it's fine."

"Okay." He picked up his slate and tapped on it for a moment, then handed it to Danny.

It appeared to be an image of Danny's lungs and abdomen, which he swiped through rather quickly until he'd seen the full set.

"Okay, but I'm not really sure what I'm looking at... or for," Danny said.

Mel resisted the urge to grab the slate and pour over the images for any anomalies, though she knew there was no way she'd see something the doctor hadn't. She stayed strong for almost thirty seconds before she held her hand out for it.

"Uh, if I may?" The doctor reached out his own hand, and Danny returned the slate to him. He paged back through to the first picture and pointed to the screen. "Here are your lungs, liver, stomach and intestines, and you can just make out your kidneys hiding out back here. Good news is that everything looks normal—there's no hemorrhaging, scarring, or other visible damage. Combined with your clean head CT, good bloodwork, and normal physical exam findings, everything suggests that you're going to be just fine." He paused. "That said, I do want to keep you here for a couple more days, just to make sure we've not missed something. Blast injuries can be tricky, so I'll feel better if I can keep an eye on you just a bit longer."

"The shorter the better, Doc," Danny said. "I've spent too long in this place already."

"We'll get you out of here as quickly as we can, I promise. Now, do either of you have any other questions?" He paused, but Mel stayed quiet and Danny shrugged. "Well, in that case, I have other patients to see. Ring a nurse if you need me."

"Thanks, Doc," Danny said.

The doctor walked to Janie's side of their shared space and pulled the curtain shut behind him.

Mel listened to their pleasantries and wondered what Janie must be feeling. Kai was here, and like it or not, this would be her world. Janie seemed happy, and if it was a facade, it was a strong one. Since Kai's arrival, Janie had been absolutely devoted, reticent to let her out of her sight even for routine checkups. Somehow, Janie was a natural—she fell right into motherhood, seemingly without effort.

*It's easy for her. Kai is all she's thought about since she got here. She was ready.* Mel's mind churned. *Can I do this? I'll never be the mother she is. How? How can I… there's no way. Oh, God!*

The baby cried out, and Janie cooed and talked to her. Moments later, the baby quieted again.

"Mel, sweetie," Danny said, "what's going on over there? You're kind of freaking me out a little."

"What?" Mel wiped unrecognized tears from her cheeks. *Guess I have my own shit to work out.*

"You kind of zoned out, then you seemed to go on some kind of Dantean descent. Are you okay?"

"Yeah, I… I'm fine."

"Okay, if you're sure." Danny said, "We're going to be okay, you know that, right? And you can talk to me. If you need to."

"Of course. I know. It's… I'm fine."

Another series of taps came from the plastic sheet door. "Hey you two, may I come in?"

*John.* Mel cringed. She'd meant to talk to him, but she hadn't left Danny's side and hadn't been able to screw up enough courage to seek him out.

"Sure, John," Danny said, "c'mon in."

"Thanks, Daniel." The door parted and John entered. "It's great to see you sort of up and talking again. I figured I'd stop by to see how you were. Sorry I haven't been by before now." He glanced at Mel, but tried not to make it obvious.

"Oh, I'm doing just fine." Danny gave her a look of his own.

John's not as subtle as he thinks.

"Doc says I'll be out of here in a couple of days, most likely," Danny continued.

"Great, that's good news," John said.

Mel got up and walked over to him. "Thanks for coming, John." She wrapped her arms around him in a hug, then stepped back to look him in the eye. "Look, I'm sorry about the other day. I freaked out and I took it out on you and you really didn't deserve all that. Will you forgive me?"

"Of course, sweetheart, I already have." He hugged her again, and it was as big and warm a hug as any they'd ever shared. "I'm just glad you both are doing better!" He let go and grinned. "And Janie!" He said in a voice loud enough to carry into the next room, "I've heard the little one is quite a hit around here!"

On the other side of the curtain, the bed creaked and cloth shuffled and a moment later Janie moved the room divider aside. She stood next to Kai in her crib. "Would you like to hold her?"

"Oh, Janie," John beamed at her. "I would love that more than anything!"

It had been a long time since Mel had seen him so happy.

## ROOM TO BREATHE

NOLAN POKED HIS HEAD THROUGH THE CURTAINS THAT SERVED as Danny's door. "So, you're back, huh? I thought you'd had enough the first time."

Mel stopped reading about plant-derived paint pigments and put down her slate.

Danny waved him in. "I do seem to keep waking up here."

"Hey Mel!" Nolan grinned and stepped through the curtains and over to Danny's bedside. "At least this time I don't have to convince them you're not going to kill everybody."

"That remains to be seen."

*Oof. There it is.* Mel said, "You didn't kill those men, Danny."

"I know that. I'm dealing. I'll be all right."

Behind the curtain, Kai stirred.

"That the baby?" Nolan asked.

Danny cast him a patronizing look. "You didn't come to see me at all, did you?"

"What? Of course I did!"

Word of Kai's birth had spread through the survivors like

sunshine. People who'd been impossible to tolerate before had mellowed out and begun to contribute. John's projects were flush with volunteers and had benefitted from a surge of progress.

"Danny, your friend can come take a peek, if he wants," Janie said from behind the curtain. "It's about time for her to eat, anyway."

Nolan's face flushed, and Mel stifled a snicker.

"You're not fooling anyone, Nolan," Danny said. "Go ahead."

Nolan pushed aside the curtain enough to get a look. After a moment, he looked back at Danny and Mel. "Oh! Danny, have you seen her? She's precious!"

"I have seen her, and she is definitely precious."

Kai fussed somewhat noncommittaly.

"Well, while you're here Mr..." Janie hesitated.

"Nolan is fine."

"While you're here, Nolan, maybe you'd like to pick her up and bring her to me?" Janie said. "Technically, I'm still not supposed to be getting her out of the crib myself, and it'll save me having to ring the nurse."

*Oh, even better!* Janie's tone prompted Mel to laugh quietly into the back of her hand.

"I, uh..." Nolan shot them another excited look. "I'd love to." He disappeared behind the curtain. Kai had worked herself up almost to the point of a good solid cry.

"Hello, little one," Nolan said. "I'm going to take you to your mommy."

Kai fell quiet, and Mel and Danny exchanged a look.

"Oh, ma'am. She's so beautiful."

"Thank you. But please Nolan, call me Janie. And this is Kai."

"Hi, Kai," Nolan stammered. "Everyone's going to be so

jealous that I got to hold her. She's all anyone can talk about. She's really something."

*Oh my god, they are so cute!* Mel grinned at Danny.

"Thank you for letting me help, Janie."

"Thank you for helping. Will you come visit us again?" she asked. "We'll be here a few more days."

"I'd love to."

As Nolan stepped back through the curtain, Danny squeezed Mel's hand. She fought not to break out laughing, and the tears in Danny's eyes said he was possibly even worse off. Nolan seemed dumbstruck as she and Danny beamed at him. It was almost too much to bear.

"What?" Nolan asked, as he broke out into his own huge grin.

---

TODAY THE GARDEN was full of life. The plants had sprouted, and the people who milled outside the entrance seemed drawn to them. Mel marveled that less than a month had passed since this place had hosted a much different crowd. Many of the same faces watched her now as they had then. Faces that would be burned into her memory forever.

Life in the cave had been hard on everyone—too hard on too many—and their victory on that previous day hadn't been an unqualified one. The fortunate few who now stood reunited with loved ones seemed almost happy. But for all those like John and herself who had taken charge of their situation, taken a stand and tried to make a difference, there were too many others who had found themselves lost in an abyss from which there seemed no escape.

The doors had closed on nearly three-thousand survivors and just over a month later they were barely over two-thousand. They were tragic losses, and since John had shared the number with her, it had never left her head.

*Seven-hundred sixty-three.*

Illness, disease, and injury had taken many; self-neglect had taken some; accidents and violence had taken far too many; but the largest losses and by far the most troubling were those who had added themselves to that tally by choice.

*Seven-hundred sixty-three.* Every one a wedge in the empty spaces in Mel's heart.

Kai's birth had changed things. It had effected everyone in some way, even Mel. People who had previously sought the comfort of communal despair now searched for light, warmth, and meaning. They rallied around John's plan and looked together toward the future. In Kai, Mel had finally regained that spark of hope she'd thought she'd lost forever.

All these things washed over Mel as she stood at the entrance to the garden, in front of this assembled crowd, and squeezed Danny's hand. Their lives would never be what she wanted, but they were here. She felt not just for herself, but for all these people. She took their every loss, every hurt, every fear, every longing, and every numb moment into herself until she could no longer say which were hers. Her eyes filled with tears, but she bit them back. *Ready.* She breathed, released Danny's hand, and stepped forward.

"Well," she said to all those expectant faces. "Here we are again."

There were a few scattered chuckles.

"First," she continued, "I want to thank those who are responsible for our being here today." She glanced behind her and gestured to John, Danny, and the other volunteers who'd helped her finish the garden. "These people gave their time and effort to realize a dream that I am happy to share now with you. Like most of us, it may not look like much—it's just a few boxes of fresh dirt and some latticework—but if you look closer, you can see new life breaking through the surface. It is my hope that this garden will stand for you as it does for me—as an emblem of hope for our future."

The crowd broke into a wave of polite applause and a few shouts of encouragement.

When the noise had died down enough for her to continue, Mel said, "Now, if you'll indulge me, there's someone I'd like to introduce."

The crowd quieted further until only the faint sounds of industry echoed from the depths of the cave. Behind Mel, the volunteers parted and Janie stepped through with little Kai cradled in her arms and Nolan at her elbow. The crowd's energy and excitement filled the cavern, though no one made a sound.

Mel turned and waved her forward. "C'mere, Janie."

She stepped up next to Mel and glanced back at Nolan, whose face shone like the sun. Mel repressed a private chuckle over her friend's rapturous appearance.

"Many of you know Janie Hartfield," Mel said, "but I'm very pleased to introduce you to her daughter, Kai."

The crowd exploded in claps, cheers, and whistles, but despite the noise, the baby barely stirred.

Mel gave Janie a hug, then turned back to address the crowd.

"So, we are here today," she said, "to dedicate this garden, not just to the memory of our lives that were, to those we've left behind, or even to those of us who survived. Even more than to those things, we are dedicating this garden to Kai and to all the children who will follow her. They represent the future—not just our future, but humanity's future. We dedicate this garden today to the joy and preciousness of life, which we can never again take for granted."

The crowd cheered, and Mel stepped back to invite them in.

Mel sang quietly as she played with Kai on the floor of Janie's unit, while Janie napped in her bedroom. Beautiful Kai smelled like an angel.

A knock on the door interrupted Mel's playful song, and she got up to answer it. She opened the door to find John and Danny who looked suspiciously pleased with themselves.

"Hey, what are you two doing here? Shouldn't you be working?" She backed up to let them in.

"Oh, we are, sweetie," Danny said.

"Can you come with us?" John asked.

"Janie's asleep, can it wait?"

"This is for Janie too. I'm fairly certain she'll want to see it."

Mel gave Danny a quizzical look, which he returned with an exasperating wink and a nod.

"Okay, then," Mel said, and turned to knock quietly on Janie's door.

Within five minutes they were downstairs, where Nolan waited beside one of the new transports that John's volunteer teams had recently constructed. Danny insisted she sit in the front, and John approached her with a long piece of gray cloth while everyone else took their seats.

"I have something to show you."

"You've taken up tie-making?"

John looked at the cloth in his hands, momentarily confused, then chuckled. "No. It's a surprise, and this is so we don't spoil it." He moved closer and lifted the cloth toward her face.

"John."

"Indulge me," he replied. "You're going to love it!"

Danny, from his seat behind her, placed a hand on her shoulder.

"Oh, all right!" she said. "But I hate surprises."

"Psh," Danny sputtered. "You love surprises."

Mel smirked, closed her eyes, and folded her hands on her lap.

"Well, go ahead then," she said.

John tied the cloth around her head, careful not to make it too tight, and Mel adjusted it for comfort when he'd finished.

The little vehicle shifted slightly as John climbed aboard, and then they were off.

As they drove, the sound opened up and closed in again as they passed each pair of buildings on either side of the avenue. She kept track until they reached the last of the main buildings, then the sound closed in once more, as though they'd entered a much smaller space. Mel desperately wanted to peek, but the tiny sliver of light that had been visible under the blindfold had gone away, so she resisted.

A minute later it sounded as though they'd entered a larger space, but not as large as the main cavern. The transport turned and slowed, then turned again and stopped. It shifted again as everyone else left their seats and shuffled around the vehicle.

John touched her hand and elbow and he helped her out of the seat and gently guided her a few steps forward, then turned her to face a particular direction.

"You can take off the blindfold now," John said.

She slipped the blindfold over her head, and after her eyes adjusted, she realized they were in the new community residential area that John and his volunteer teams had worked so hard the last month to build. Plain gray buildings, made from cinder block or something like it, protruded a few feet out from the natural cave wall. The construction was like the buildings in the main cavern, but on a smaller scale.

As relatively normal as that first glance seemed within the context of the cave, portions of the scene in front of her descended almost into absurdity. The building she faced had windows on either side of a central door framed by what appeared to be decorative shutters, painted dark gray, almost black. The door itself—painted a deep navy blue—looked for all the world like someone had picked it up from a nearby hardware store. It was nearly perfect in every detail. The whole thing was ridiculously quaint, but irresistibly adorable. There were other things too, and as Mel took them all in, her breath caught in her throat. *No.* She recognized it. It was not exactly, but astonishingly close to the updates her mother had made to their house after Dad died. The similarity to the home in which she'd spent so many years was striking.

John beamed at her while Danny grinned impishly and shrugged his shoulders. A second door, offset more toward the side of the structure, was the same dark blue.

"John," she finally said, "This is **adorable**! You did this?"

"Well, I had help, of course," he replied. "A family needs a home, and to feel like they're doing more than just surviving. Living up there was only ever going to feel like surviving. Down here we can start to build a real community."

Mel looked around the cave, which seemed to be bathed in sunlight. Many buildings of the same general construction sat along both sides, though none were so elaborately decorated. If not for the cave walls, this could have been the final phase of a new subdivision of patio homes. Farther into the cave a second level of buildings sat a meter or so above the others and behind a railed balcony. The buildings themselves were plain, but taken together their effect was striking. She wondered if she'd ever get used to it, but already felt it tug at her heart.

Janie and Nolan, with Kai, stood in front of the next building, arm in arm. They talked and laughed animatedly. Janie smiled sweetly when she noticed Mel's attention, and Mel's heart sang for her friend's happiness.

Mel imagined the space filled with people, a real neighborhood. It was more of an innocuous vision than a comforting one, but she knew it would be enough.

"Thank you, John." She hugged him and held on.

"This is our home now," he said, and brought Danny into their embrace. "Let's make the best of it." He broke free and gently pushed them toward it. "In ya go."

# ACKNOWLEDGMENTS

As with most good things in life, writing is rarely a truly solo endeavor. Time and space are needed for the creative process, and attention and collaboration are needed to turn the creative output into something that might appeal to the above-average person.

It goes without saying that I owe a great deal to my incomparable wife, Sara, who is my protector of space and time, my encourager, and my first reader. None of this would be possible without her support.

Gifts of time and space—the most valuable commodity for a father-of-three—were also graciously provided by my mother-in-law Teresa on many occasions expressly to allow me to pursue this work.

Early on, after my initial efforts of "winging it" failed, my friend Nathan helped break the story and nail down the outline that kept me on track while finishing the first draft.

My friend Paul kindly gave me notes on an early draft, and a very strong group of readers dug deep into subsequent drafts, providing copious, well considered notes. Hunter, Nick, Bob, Devon, Garrett, David, Jennifer, and my sister Sara are those valued souls to whom I am extremely grateful. My editor Alida Winternheimer also provided a very detailed critique which helped focus and strengthen the book into what it is today.

In recent years, I've been joined on this journey by my honored patrons Cori, Danny B, Sharon, Chris G, Steven & Ruthie, Dawn, and Chris B., who have pledged and provided support and encouragement as I continue to bring this story to life. I am extremely grateful to have such a devoted group of fans, friends, and family.

To all of these people and more who read or expressed interest in my work, I offer my humble and profound thanks.

# ABOUT THE AUTHOR

When I was seven, I wanted to be an astronaut. Or, perhaps more accurately, I wanted to be Buck Rogers. At thirteen, I wanted to be a fighter pilot, or a helicopter pilot, or, perhaps more accurately, I wanted to be Stringfellow Hawke behind the stick of Airwolf.

Growing up in a small town, with limited opportunities and seemingly stagnant aspirations, it seemed that even these more mundane goals—astronaut or pilot—were so far out of my reach as to be practically unattainable.

Their impracticality did nothing to hamper my enjoyment of science, astronomy, or stories about space travel and fantastical adventures. I still wanted to be Captain Kirk, living in an idealistic utopia built on human brotherhood, enabled by scientific advances, and bound by dispassionate but compassionate logic.

As an adult, I've realized how much the stories we enjoy inform and shape our lives. And I've seen how impractical idealism isn't an end unto itself, but rather it is, in the Buddhist vernacular, the finger pointing at the moon.

Story—be it fiction, non-fiction, news and opinion, music, or art—can provide a taste of euphoria, a dose of fear, the thrum of tension, or the pull of love, and can point us in the direction of a better life and a better world, if we only listen.

That's the goal—to point an idealistic finger toward the moon of a better world. One day I'll get there, and in the meantime, I'll tell the best stories I can, and hope they meet you wherever you find them.

# ALSO AVAILABLE

*When storms and ash drive Earth's survivors underground, settlers on Mars find themselves in a whole new fight for survival.*

## *Inheritance of Dust*
### A *Rogue Planet* novella

*They chose a world of struggle and dust.*

*Will their hope hold when tragedy strikes?*

Leana chased bold dreams toward humanity's future on an unforgiving Mars. The first settlers' joyous new beginning is shattered when Earth's catastrophe leaves them racing for survival amid struggles for power and control. Can Leana help them rise above despair and an indifferent planet to leave their children more than martian dust?

Learn more here: https://mattr.space/iod

*Our Once Warm Earth* and *Inheritance of Dust* are novella-length excerpts from the near-future sci-fi post-apocalypse novel *The Severed Sky* which will soon be recombined and published as a single volume.

# THE JOURNEY CONTINUES

If you enjoyed this story, I'd love to share more like it with you.

Follow the ongoing development of the *Rogue Planet* series, keep up-to-date with future stories, go behind-the-scenes, and learn more about me and my writing by joining the crew today.

https://mattr.space/join/oowe

As a thank you, I'll send you a link to my Starter Collection which includes two free sci-fi short stories that expand on the world and events of *The Severed Sky*.

FOR MORE FROM *THE SEVERED SKY* **RIGHT NOW**,

PLEASE ENJOY THE FOLLOWING EXCERPT.

*Sol 718, 9 pm*
*20°0'S 356°35'E*
*Zubrin Crater, Mars*

Dust devils glided across the crater floor as the last drop fell into Leana's glass. Luis sat the bottle on the counter, picked up his own glass, and clinked hers in an unspoken toast. They leaned against the counter and sipped their drinks.

"I miss wine," Leana said as she swirled the contents in her glass.

"A few more months," Luis said. "As soon as it's ready, I'll make sure you have some." He set his glass on the counter, wrapped his arms around her, and nestled his face against hers. "Homemade grape juice isn't the same, but let's not forget that this is very special… the first-ever Martian grape juice from the first-ever Martian grapes."

She loved the smell of him, the warmth of his cheek against hers. Mars may be breathtaking, but after all this time, he could still take hers away.

"True," she said, and smiled.

She treasured these moments—early evening with the children asleep and the day's work complete—when they could finally be together. This was when it felt most like Earth, felt like it had when they'd just started out, just fallen in love—when they'd first planned to be exactly here. The day, the work, and the place fell away, and all that mattered was that they were together.

Tonight felt different, though. After two years with just the four of them here, tonight was the last night they'd be able to say with any confidence that they were the only people awake on the entire planet. Tomorrow, everything would change. Everything they'd worked toward over the last decade would finally begin.

His dream had brought them here, but their love had made it possible. "I couldn't do this without you, you know."

"And I'd be lost without you." He said.

"So true." She flashed him a mischievous smile, and he looked at her in that way she loved. A warm flush rose in her chest and she turned to him, took his glass, and placed it in the sink with her own. "I'll get them in the morning." She took his hand. "Let's go to bed."

---

# CONTENT WARNING

*Our Once Warm Earth* contains scenes that may be upsetting to some readers.

Specific content warnings include depictions of natural disaster, personal violence, bodily injury, death, and suicide.

In the United States, anyone experiencing a suicidal crisis or emotional distress should call the National Suicide Prevention Lifeline at 1-800-273-8255.